Disclaimer

By the same author

The Miracle of Bean's Bullion
The Mouse Cricket Caper
The Indian Mouse Cricket Caper
The Mystery of the Goodfellowes' Code

Bonzo the Wonder Dog and the Cricket World Cup

By Mark Trenowden

2019 Edition

ISBN 978-1-5272-3846-6

Cover by Steven Johnson

www.steillustrates.co.uk

Thanks to Anna Bowles for your editing and Rikin Parehk for your splendid Bonz

Dotball Books

Halifax, Nova Scotia, Canada

BONZO THE WONDER DOG AND THE CRICKET WORLD CUP

Mark Trenowden

DotBall

Table of Contents

Chapter 1 – The Toolbox Gang

Sitting at a red traffic light in a lane of the South Circular on the outskirts of London, Reggie Paynter reflected on the day's events. What a day it had been, he thought as he patted the steering wheel of Speedy', his Morris Minor convertible. Together they had won the 'best in class' category at the Pratts Bottom Historic Vehicle Show.

Speedy was so named not because there was a supercharged engine under its immaculately polished green bonnet, but because of its registration number, SPD 111. The car had passed through many owners during its lifetime. However, despite being over fifty years old it seemed to be in showroom condition. Reggie was used to comments from passing admirers, particularly if he had the top down, like today. A quirky-looking youth with a blond mullet of bubble curls appeared to be taking an interest now.

'Oi, Grandad!' the youth called from the pavement. 'Is your mota supposed to be making all that blue smoke?'
'Smoke?' Reggie queried, cupping his hand to his ear. He checked in his rear-view mirror and skipped out of the car to take a look at the exhaust pipe.

It was the oldest trick in the book and Reggie had fallen for it. Before he had time to react the youth had jumped in through the passenger door and slid across to the driver's seat. The light turned green, and the youth floored the accelerator. Reggie grabbed feebly at the faultlessly shined chrome bumper as the car pulled away. As Speedy disappeared into the distance, he was left standing speechless in the road.

Inside the car, the youth known as Muppet slunk as low down into the red leather driver's seat as he could. Stealing an old bloke's car was pretty despicable, and the injustice of it wasn't lost on him. However, he'd been given a job to do, and it was a dog-eat-dog world out there. Billy Murphy – Muppet's real name – had been recently recruited to the Tooting 'Toolbox' gang.

'We need a car for Tuesday night's job,' Jago O'Toole had told him. He was a thick-set man with hard features, hollow cheeks and a ruddy complexion He had the look of a man for whom life had been a struggle but who'd wrestled it as best he could. Not the type to argue with or ask too many questions.

'Yeah, make sure it's a good'un with plenty of umpf,' his brother Finn had chimed in. Finn had an altogether less threatening demeanour. A bigger, fleshier face with rosy cheeks. He looked more suited to rural life than ducking and diving in the grimier parts of the city. His softer personality and more breezy approach to life often diffused tense situations.

Muppet had considered the demands. It wasn't what he'd signed up for as a driver, not that there was any official documentation to sign. Driving was one thing; pinching things was another. In fact, it would be true to say that he'd been on the point of pulling out of the job altogether. It wasn't as though he'd done anything like it before. How did you go about stealing a car? He'd take the telling-off, he reasoned. Wear the accompanying slap that Jago was all too quick to hand out and perhaps live to fight another day. But then, just when the mission had seemed impossible, the little green car had presented itself. Alone at a traffic light with just a little old guy behind the wheel.

Before he knew it, he found himself forming the words. The driver had fallen for the trick and stepped out of the car without protest. In an instant, Muppet was sitting behind the wheel, and the lights had changed. He glanced over his shoulder at the owner receding into the distance, and for a moment he felt a pang of guilt. Should he pull over, walk away, leave the keys in the ignition and the engine running? Then a mental image of Jago's face, contorted in snarling anger, clouded his thoughts. Automatically he signalled and turned left off the busy road. He threaded his way through the back streets of Streatham and Balham, and on to Tooting.

At the end of a residential street, he pulled into a driveway, its surface broken and sprinkled with tufts of grassy weeds. At the end of it stood four garages with grubby shutters shedding flakes of paint. He pulled out his phone and called Jago.

'Whatcha,' he ventured nervously.

'I hope this is good news,' Jago replied tersely.

'Yeah, I'm at the lock-up now. You coming down?'

'We sure are. We'll see you in an hour or so.'

'OK.' Muppet tried to sound as upbeat as possible, though he wasn't thrilled to have to hang around the garages for so long. He busied himself in working out how to put the car's soft roof back up. It was a tricky business but eventually he was satisfied with the result. While he waited, he slumped moodily in the driver's seat and played a game on his phone.

It was some time before he heard voices. The two brothers had parked in the street and walked the length of the driveway. He slipped out of the car and was just lowering the shutter to the ground as they approached.

'Hold up!' cried, Finn. 'Don't go shutting up shop before we've had a butcher's.'

Muppet looked nonplussed.

'Butcher's hook... look.' Jago clarified matters.

'Err... no, obviously,' Muppet stammered. 'It's just that...' His words trailed off as Jago took a step towards him.

'It's just what?'

'It's just that the car may not be entirely what you had in mind.'

'Here Finn, it sounds as though the *Muppet* –' he stressed the nickname – 'has a surprise for us. And you know I don't like surprises.' There was an ominous note in Jago's voice.

'I did what you said. I got a car. I didn't get caught. Nobody got hurt.' Muppet was almost pleading.

Jago was going to take no more of this. 'Do the honours, will you, Finnegan?' He motioned to the garage. Finn did as he was asked and pushed the garage door back in one fluent motion. There stood the compact old green car with its curvy lines. Both men struggled to hide their disbelief at what, in Muppet's eyes, constituted a getaway car.
'Oh my good gawd, you have got to be kiddin' me,' Jago exclaimed, reeling away. He circled the forecourt, one hand pressed to his forehead, muttering to himself. Finn, always keen to ingratiate himself with his brother, started on Muppet.

'You've done it now.'

'Look!' Muppet put up both his hands as he pleaded his case. 'It's a nice clean car, reliable and surprisingly nippy.'

'I don't care if Lewis blooming Hamilton has been driving it,' Finn batted back. 'It ain't big enough for Tuesday's job. It's a jewellers' we're knocking off, not a Smarties factory.'

'It's got a boot,' Muppet pointed out.

'Boot? I'll give you a boot if you don't watch out.'

'The job's off.' Jago joined the conversation. 'Simple as...' The words were intended to sting and threaten. He stepped towards Muppet, not stopping until they were nose to nose. 'As for you, young man, you are in TROUBLE. You owe me, BIG time. You got that?'

'Yes, Jago,' Muppet replied, his eyes downcast.

'Now get out of my sight, before I lose my temper,' Jago barked.

'I'm sorry, Jago, Finn...' Muppet pleaded.
'GET...!' The brothers roared in unison.

Muppet took to his heels and ran off down the driveway. Then he kept running. He ran for all he was worth until he felt safe.

Chapter 2 – An Incredibly Unfortunate Occurrence

'We are the champions, WE ARE THE CHAMPIONS!' Mr Bradfield softly roared the last line under his breath. It was as though he was belting out the Queen anthem to an adoring crowd. This was an unseen side to the librarian and curator of the Lord's Museum collection.

It's curious that some of the things held in highest esteem can, in the cold light of day, appear startlingly ordinary. Take for example the exit from the grounds of Buckingham Palace. One moment you're in the Queen's back garden, the next you've stepped through a large wooden gate and are standing at a bus stop on Grosvenor Place, London SW1.

The same might be said of the carpet-covered stairs that lead down from the library at Lord's Cricket Ground. Stairs that wouldn't look out of place in any home in the land. However ordinary their appearance, Mr Bradfield descended them on this day with a spring in his step. The famous club's cricket history guru paused and checked his reflection in the glass of a framed photograph. He flattened his beard to his face with both palms and continued on his way.

At one of the entrances to the ground stood a small man. The Grace Gates, erected to commemorate the bearded W.G. Grace, loomed behind him as he waited to be met. At his feet rested a large, rectangular silver aluminium suitcase. To anyone with an overactive imagination or a taste for James Bond films, he might well have passed for a hitman. In reality, his role, although it did have a sprinkling of international mystery, was less exciting.

Once the announcement of the schedule for the Cricket World Cup had been made, Mr Bradfield had received a call.

'We will be making the trophy available for promotional purposes in the build-up to the competition,' a representative of the Global Cricket Board informed him. 'Lord's, the home of Cricket would be a fitting place for it to be kept.' True to their word, their trusty courier had been dispatched, and now he had arrived at Lord's.

'Mr Saad,' Mr Bradfield called out with a wave. 'I hope you had a good trip.'

'Yes, very scenic, thank you,' Mr Saad grinned revealing a large gap between his front teeth.

'I hope you're not jet-lagged.'

'No, not at all, it isn't too long a flight from Dubai, and we're only three hours ahead of you guys. But I've actually been here a couple of days already.' Mr Saad added inscrutably.

'Oh, really?'

'Yes, I've been in Kent at the silversmiths who originally made the trophy. They've been giving it a nice wash and brush-up before I hand it over.'

'How interesting: it lives at the offices of the GCB overseas, but it was created here in the UK,' Bradfield observed. 'Perhaps if you follow me I'll show you where its home is going to be for the next few months.'

Mr Bradfield showed Mr Saad the way with a flourish, and the two men walked the short distance to the Lord's Museum. There was a definite end-of-cricket-season feeling to the goings-on around the stadium. A couple of paint-splattered decorators had parked their van and were inspecting a potential job.

'I'm greatly looking forward to seeing the Ashes Urn,' Mr Saad ventured conversationally.

'Oh no, what a shame. I'm afraid it is in Australia at the moment,' Mr Bradfield replied with a grin.

'I don't believe it! The first time I come to Lord's, and I find its most iconic piece is elsewhere.' Mr Saad's wide-eyed horror was a reaction his host hadn't intended.

'I'm only kidding,' Mr Bradfield exclaimed with a playful push that he instantly regretted given Mr Saad's latest grimace. 'Of course it's here. The last time it went anywhere, to my knowledge, was in 2006. And you can imagine –' he indicated Mr Saad's own burden – 'the effort that went into that little undertaking.'

Mr Saad whipped out a large handkerchief from his breast pocket and wiped his brow in mock-relief.

'Given your interest, I think you'll be delighted with the arrangements I've made for your trophy,' went on Mr Bradfield.

The images conjured up by the word 'museum' depend on who you ask. For some, perhaps unconsciously, it evokes an image of musty, dark, oak-panelled rooms, home to faded items of dubious interest. You're more likely to find clean-cut lines and open, well-lit areas in museums of today. Spaces that are cleverly planned, with items carefully sourced and displayed.

The Lord's Museum is a mixture of both these approaches. Thanks to a glazed roof it is a light, airy space. However, due to the nature of the game it celebrates a number of the exhibits on display, are frankly, a bit tired, even sweaty, and in some cases worm-holed and moth-eaten. But only a heathen would categorise the caps worn for many seasons by W.G. Grace as moth-eaten. Perhaps stumps from memorable games are treated for woodworm, and Don Bradman wore Odor-Eaters in his boots.

However, the Lord's collection is constantly evolving, moving forward. One player reaching a milestone, another retiring from the international game. A Test series win or a County triumph in a domestic competition. Each one of these creates images, soundtracks and memorabilia to be collected, recorded and displayed. This is where the curator and his expertise come to the fore.

The 2018 touring sides of Pakistan and India both had their own dedicated displays that drew on the museum's reserves of items of interest, from Imran Khan to Sachin Tendulkar. But, long before the last ball of the Oval Test between England and India had been bowled, Mr Bradfield had been dismantling the displays in his mind. Paintings were being stored into the Lord's archive and cricket curios squirreled away. All this while dreaming up a suitable setting for the Cricket World Cup.

'Morning, Mr Bradfield.' The steward on duty at the entrance to the museum greeted him with a nod.' Go right in, you have the place to yourselves.'

The two men entered the ground floor of the museum. A calm and ordered space with an airy feel. Glass-fronted cabinets flanked each side, housing some of the museum's key items of memorabilia. Bats, caps, blazers, trophies. As varied as Shane Warne's plaster cast from a broken wrist to a stuffed sparrow hit by a ball in 1936.

'We're going this way.' Mr Bradfield motioned towards a set of stairs in the centre of the room. 'Our little urn is up there.'

Mr Saad followed. At one end of the first floor, in a glass cube, stood the Ashes Urn, its profile unmistakable.

Mr Saad drew in a breath before exclaiming, 'There she is...'

'Yes, Mr Saad, and if you look just across the way, there is a second cabinet for your cup. Pride of place, one might say.'

'Ahh, that is very fine,' Mr Saad purred.

Together the two men made their way over to the cabinets. Mr Saad gave the Ashes Urn a thorough examination.

'It really is so small,' he observed. 'But such a potent symbol of the rivalry between England and Australia.'

'Right on both counts, sir,' Mr Bradfield agreed. 'Now what about that other trophy we'd like to get our hands on?'

Mr Saad laid his case on the floor and clicked open the catches. He offered Mr Bradfield a pair of white cotton gloves and put on a pair himself. Suitably attired, he bent down and respectfully lifted the Cricket World Cup. Mr Bradfield stepped forward to help him, as the cup was quite a solid item. Sixty centimetres of gold and silver; three columns of stumps and bails supporting a globe-like ball.

'Ahh, magnificent,' Mr Bradfield crowed.

'If you could get the door?'

Mr Bradfield opened the hinged door of the cabinet. Mr Saad was just about to place the cup inside it when his phone rang in his pocket.

'Oh no, I should get that, I'm expecting an important call,' Mr Saad exclaimed, suddenly flustered.

'No problem,' said Mr Bradfield, holding out his hands to take the cup. For a moment Mr Saad seemed reluctant to let it go, but then passed it over. He retrieved his phone and went on a distracted walkabout as he took the call.

'Hello...? Hello...?' he barked into the handset. 'Hello?'

'The signal is always terrible in here. You're better off outside,' Mr Bradfield explained. Mr Saad nodded his understanding and made his way down the stairs and out of the building.

For the second time that day Mr Bradfield contemplated his reflection. He provided a suitable soundtrack by exclaiming, 'The winners of this year's Cricket World Cup... ENGLAND!' In his mind's eye, an ecstatic crowd cried out for its presentation. Mr Bradfield duly obliged, lifting it above his shoulders and giving it a good shake. As he did so there was a clearly audible... *Plink*!

Mr Bradfield did a spectacular double-take, and his eyebrows climbed up his forehead in dismay. Not only did it sound like he'd broken the trophy but, he suddenly realised, at eleven kilos it was quite heavy. He staggered towards the cabinet and put it down with a thud. Spinning it on its polished base, he inspected it for damage. 'Nooo!' He sucked in a horrified breath. There it was. Tiny, almost imperceptible... A crack where one of the bails met the band running around the globe.

Mr Saad arrived back from his call.

'How does it look?'

'Just fine and dandy,' Mr Bradfield told the teeniest white lie.

'Let me have a closer look.'

'I wouldn't do that if I were you,' Mr Bradfield barked, leaping between Mr Saad and the cabinet.

'My dear fellow, what's got into you?'

'Nothing, it's just that I'm so excited to have the trophy here.' He grabbed the astonished Mr Saad by both hands and proceeded to dance around in circles.

'Put me down!' he pleaded. Mr Bradfield let go of his guest. As Mr Saad tried to regain his composure the museum's curator tried another diversionary tactic.

'There goes my phone.'

'No, it doesn't.'

'Err, yes, I heard it quite distinctly.' Mr Bradfield rummaged in his pocket for his phone and put it to his ear. 'Yes, Bradfield here,' he paused as if listening to the fictional caller. 'Really? Oh my goodness. REALLY!' he stressed the word. 'Yes, okay, right away, goodbye, thank you.'

'Who was it?' Mr Saad looked concerned.

'Security,' he replied simply.' It seems something has tripped the museum's alarm system. The security staff need to evacuate the building to investigate.'

'Surely we...'

'Come along now, chop chop. We have to do as we're told, I'm afraid.' With that, he marched Mr Saad down the stairs. The visitor tried to get a last glimpse of the cup as he passed.

'Well, I've never been so...'

'A thousand apologies, Mr Saad. What can I say, I'm so sorry. This is all most embarrassing.'

Mr Saad raised a questioning eyebrow. Mr Bradfield's odd behaviour was not going unnoticed.

'As it happens, I need to be heading off to the airport now anyway. I have to say that I'm not happy with the way you have conducted yourself, sir. I will be making a report to my seniors. Make no mistake –' he wagged his finger under Mr Bradfield's nose – 'we'll be monitoring things from our offices in Dubai, and if anything happens to the World Cup, you will be held personally responsible.'

Mr Bradfield swallowed hard and adjusted his tie.

'Absolutely. I will do my utmost to see that nothing untoward happens to the trophy.'

'You had better, or else.' Mr Saad delivered the ultimatum in what Mr Bradfield felt was a rather ominous tone.

Chapter 3 – It Had Been a Funny Old Summer

Hybrid is a word that we encounter more and more. It can refer to plants, cars, renewable energy so why not dogs. A cockapoo, is just that, a hybrid dog, a cross between a cocker spaniel and a poodle. They are smart, even-tempered and don't drop their hair. They've become a popular choice for many families keen to have a pooch to pamper. The Khan's of Clapham, South London had followed that trend. They had welcomed Bonzo, a compact black and white version of the hybrid breed into their home.

Bonzo had not disappointed. He was great with the children. Fun and loveable and relatively easy to train. With every day that passed, he'd become a much loved, fully- fledged member of the family.

Despite all that love, there was one part of every day when, as far as Bonzo, was concerned, his people abandoned him. At 'bedtime,' as they called it, there would be much cooing and stroking and kind words. His bed would be plumped up, and his friend Cyril (did they not know that he wasn't real?) would be placed beside him. Actually, Cyril was all right. Bonzo was fond of him. But he was just a stuffed toy with googly eyes and a small hole where his insides were coming out.

At 'bedtime', the local fox population was on the prowl, too. When Bonzo was taken for his last late-night wee, he could already smell that they'd been about. Pulling at rubbish bags or scavenging a discarded fried-chicken box. That was the sort of behaviour that would earn *him* a short, sharp reprimand. Life just wasn't fair. Oh well, he'd have to make do with his fuzzy bed in his safe home with its love and regular meals.

It was the first week of September and the early morning light spilling through the doors to the garden had woken him. He'd been lying in his bed listening for any movement that suggested his lonely night-time vigil was at an end. His people were getting back into a familiar routine, he could tell that from the preparations they'd been making the night before. The children's bags had been put out and his dad – actually everyone's dad, Anwar – had brought the bicycles into the kitchen from the garden shed. He knew all the signs, they'd soon be back into their daily routine. It had been a while, the children had been around for many days, but Bonzo knew what to expect now. He just had to be patient.

Somewhere in the upper regions of the house he sensed a stirring. It was Jen, his mum, he guessed, as she was usually the first up. Yes, he recognised her tread. Bonzo waited. The clonk of the door, a pause, the rush of water. Eventually it came to an end. The clonk of the door again. Then whoosh, occasionally the children blew hot air on him with the thing that made that noise.

A moment's silence then finally, the sound of her descending the stairs. *Right, action!* Bonzo thought to himself. He'd stay cool for just a moment longer. As Jen approached the kitchen door, he raised an eye, the white of it showing around the shiny brown pupil... and...

Good morning, good morning, I love you, I love you, where have you been? Why were you gone for so long? All these greetings spilled out of him, expressed only by his energetic bouncing at his owner's feet.

'Oh, Bonzo, good morning. Have you been a good boy? Did you see those naughty foxes?'

Yes, I did see those foxes, and you're right they're very naughty, he thought.

'Is it lunchtime?' Jen asked him.

Yes, it jolly well is lunchtime. You know that! he thought. For Bonzo, every meal was called lunchtime. He recognised the intonation as well as having the most precise body clock known to man or dog.

As Jen put Bonzo's food down, Anwar made an appearance. This threw Bonzo into a quandary. Should he eat, or go through the whole welcoming performance again?

There was an unspoken handover of duties. Jen passed Anwar on her way upstairs to get ready for work, a slice of toast in one hand and mug of tea in the other. Anwar worked from home and so the job of getting the children to school fell to him.

'The kids awake?' she grunted.

'Sort of,' Anwar replied, giving his tousled black curly hair a scratch. His style fell into the 'relaxed' category, his scruffy T-shirt and boxer shorts giving him a youthful appearance. He was easy-going and a cool dad, but this tended to backfire on him when trying to be the boss.

There followed a period where the hapless Anwar coaxed, delivered ultimatums, pleaded and eventually got the kids down to breakfast.

'May we have *Milkshake* on?' Lita asked.

He negotiated the tricky 'Do we, don't we?' question of allowing telly at breakfast. It provided an incentive to the kids on the one hand, with a potential delay on the other.

The next hurdle was the return upstairs to undertake the process of dressing, with the many potential pitfalls that provided.

'Have a great day and be good for Daddy,' Jen called from the front door as she left for her office.

Anwar called back an undecipherable response from the bathroom where he had a mouthful of toothpaste. He spat it out and called again, 'Guys, you've got ten minutes... I want you dressed, teeth cleaned, school bags, the lot. See you down there.'

Anwar jogged down the stairs. The problem with living in a terrace was that everything from the back garden had to come through the house. The morning transfer of bikes along the narrow hallway to the front door was an awkward, frustrating and sometimes painful chore. A crushed finger or skinned shin was almost guaranteed. Zak, ten, and Lita, eight, joined him as he fed the first of the bikes out of the front door.

'Grab this will you, son?' Anwar asked as he pushed Zak's bike out to him. Zak, a 'mini-me' version of Anwar, obliged.

Lita followed him out.

'Did you brush your hair at all?'

'I used my tangle-tamer,' Lita replied indignantly. Her dark eyes flashed a look at her father from beneath her unruly hair.

The matter settled the two children waited patiently on the small paved area by their gate. Anwar paired them up with their school bags and packed lunches. The push-me-pull-you morning drama of fretting, things lost, excuses and arguments was complete and forgotten.

'GOOD MORNING!' a voice bellowed. It was Loud Dunc, their New Zealand neighbour who was also on his way out. It was hard to imagine a man more upbeat and, well, loud. 'The first day back to school, eh? New school bags... GRAYYT!' he enthused. The children smiled their reply. They were never quite sure what to make of Loud Dunc. He beamed back at them and with a wave strode off to the Tube station.

Anwar fed his bike through the door, attached Bonzo to his lead and then ushered the Khan family party out of the gate. With this action they joined a small army of mums, dads and commuters converging on Clapham Common. This area of London was known as Nappy Valley because of its concentration of young families.

The Khans made their way to the top of their road. Things were busier here as they joined the main thoroughfare. The children expertly wove their way through the crowd of people and Anwar followed just behind with Bonzo, on his lead, trotting happily beside him. They negotiated a zebra crossing, a striped tongue that fed into the mouth of the Tube station.

'Hold up, kids, I just need to pop into Dolly and Tushar's shop.'

'I wanna come too,' Lita demanded.

They left Zak minding the bikes propped up against the local newsagents.

'Morning, you two.' Dolly the shopkeeper greeted them warmly. The shop was busy, and they joined a short queue at the counter. In front of them, a youth with a mass of blond curly hair shifted his weight impatiently from foot to foot. His hand hovered over the display in front of the counter. As if he thought himself invisible, he scrunched a bag of Chocolate Buttons into his fist. Lita watched in a mixture of wide-eyed amazement and outrage.

'Dad, that man has just taken something,' she announced bluntly. Muppet, for it was he, dropped the Buttons as though they were electrified.

'WHAT?' he wailed in feigned outrage.

'Out you go,' Dolly scolded.

'Come on, push off, mate.' Anwar joined the little band of local law enforcement.

'I ain't dun nuffink,' Muppet protested, knowing the game was up. 'Keep yer smelly sweets,' he added, before bolting through the door.

'YAY us!' Anwar cried, high-fiving Lita.

'It happens all the time,' Dolly moaned, shaking her head.

Outside, Muppet paused for a moment. Bonzo took one look at him, decided he was worth a good bark and duly obliged.

'Hey, Bonz, cool it.' Zak calmed him.

'We had an adventure,' Lita announced as they re-joined Zak and the dog.

'He wouldn't have had something to do with it by any chance?' Zak nodded in the direction of Muppet, who was mooching off. 'Come, on you can tell me all about it as we walk.'

Anwar led the party over two roads via traffic islands. This brought them up to a leafy cinder path, where they bumped into some friends.

'Happy new term! How is everyone?' called out the mum, Andrea. She had just gone through the same process as Anwar and was pleased to see another adult. Her sons Vinny and Oski were carrying scooters over their shoulders.

The two groups merged, and Vinny and Oski made a big fuss of Bonzo.

'We saw him in the paper,' Vinny said giving Bonzo a stroke. The stocky little dog licked his hand, and Vinny stroked him again, from the top of his head, down his woolly back and ending at the top of the white plume of his tail.

'Our local wonder dog,' Andrea joked. 'We have nowt oop North like him.' She put on a jokey accent.

'You had a good summer in Yorkshire with your mum?' Anwar asked.

'Yes, the children love her caravan, and it's great to get out of London. I was forgetting, we haven't really seen you since the end of term.'

'Yeah, we've kinda kept busy,' Anwar replied vaguely. 'You know, doing... stuff.'

'I know all about your "stuff", as you call it.' She turned her attention to Bonzo, bending down to his level, and put on a dog-friendly voice. 'We've heard all about you. You're such a clever boy.'

Bonzo winked. Not just a blink, but a clear one-eyed wink. 'Did you see that?' asked an astonished Andrea.

'Did Bonzo wink at you?' asked Lita. 'He does that.' She said it as if it was the most normal thing in the world.

The end of the summer term had turned the local spotlight to Bonzo in an unexpected way. Some of the parents had decided to have a picnic on the common. They'd chosen a grassy spot near the Chuck Wagon, a van that sold snacks and wasn't run by any Chuck but by a bloke called Bob. It was a permanent fixture on Windmill Drive. This was the road that cut through the common, and so was a landmark everyone knew.

It had been a great afternoon. A perfect combination of getting the children out of doors, keeping them entertained and feeding them. They'd enjoyed playing games in the big grassy space, and the July sunshine. Bonzo had also had a lovely time, with multiple playmates some of them human and some of the doggy variety. He'd had a steady supply of willing ball-throwers, and he'd pretty much run himself to a standstill.

Some of the children had started playing cricket. There seemed to be multiple balls in play. Bonzo watched as his favourite ball was hit through the railings, coming to rest by the Chuck Wagon. Wearily he raised himself and trotted over to rescue it.

The ball had rolled off the pavement and come to rest in the gutter at one end of the wagon. Bonzo tried to scrabble it out, but his paws couldn't get a grip on it.

Inside the wagon, after years of excellent service, Bob's hot plate was malfunctioning. Beneath the counter, the heatproof panel had come loose. As it no longer deflected the heat, the side wall of the wagon was being cooked at the same time as the burgers. Gradually, a blackened spot had become a glow and was now just starting to ignite. Above Bonzo smoke had begun to curl out from the side of the wagon.

Oblivious to this, he continued to paw at the ball. As he got increasingly frustrated a whine turned to a yelp and then a bark.

Bob, who was just handing a hot dog to a customer, leaned out of the wagon.

'What has got into that mutt?' he asked.

'Don't know, looks like he's found something,' the customer replied vaguely, distracted by the process of squeezing a worm of tomato sauce onto his lunch.

Bob, whose five-star hygiene rating didn't include dogs sniffing about his wagon, let himself out of the back and walked round to shoo Bonzo away. He was met by the sight of smoke billowing out of the side of the wagon.

'OH MY GAWD!' he yelled. 'FIRE! FIRE! Quick, someone call the fire brigade!'

As he did so, Bonzo finally retrieved his ball and ran back to join his people.

'BACK, EVERYONE GET BACK!' Bob shouted, running onto the grass. 'THE GAS CYLINDER IS GOING TO BLOW!'
As everyone had a mobile phone, a 999 call drew a speedy response from the fire brigade in Clapham Old Town. They were less than a mile away and in no time at all they'd arrived.

The sight of a fully-fledged, shiny red fire engine at close quarters was very exciting. It arrived complete with its full range of 'blues and twos' – lights and siren. An added bonus was that the children had met the firefighters on a school visit, so this wasn't a potential disaster, it was a community event. The firefighters acted swiftly. They liberally doused the wagon with foam and order was restored.

Poor Bob, still wearing his apron, surveyed his smoking livelihood, hands on hips. A paramedic in a dark green jumpsuit made his way over to him.

'Do you need to sit down, mate? You're probably a bit shocked.'

'No, I'm all right, thanks. I got out because that little dog over there started barking. A sort of warning, I guess.'

Bonzo, who had found some shade, was having a good gnaw of his ball. He was oblivious to the compliment being paid him.

Soon the news of Bonzo's timely intervention spread. Bob approached the Khan family to tell them about the unlikely hero, and Zak and Lita called him over. 'He deserves a medal, I think,' Bob said, giving Bonzo a pat.' That could have turned very nasty, very nasty indeed.' He rubbed his chin thoughtfully.

So Bonzo gained celebrity status, which rose to the heady heights of a couple of column inches and a slightly fuzzy photograph in the *Wandsworth Gazette*. The children badgered their dad to start an Instagram account for him. For almost a week they had a minor local celebrity on their hands.

Gradually the summer holidays played out. Friends went away one by one on package holidays. Bob's insurance kicked in, and the repaired Chuck Wagon returned to business.

And now here they all were again, back on the walk across Clapham Common. The comfort of routine restored. (How many crossings did a person make in their school career? Two a day would add up to a lot. The children rode their bikes down the bike path, and Anwar bumped across the still sun-baked grass, giving Bonzo a run. The speedometer on his bike told him that Bonzo's cruising speed was about eight miles an hour.

They all came together to cross the last road. After that, the children went on ahead to catch up with friends as everyone waited outside the school for it to open.

There had been a bit more Bonzo fuss as they waited outside the school. Everyone wanted to give him a pat and have their picture taken with him. Anwar pushed a weary hand through his hair. Getting back into the saddle of the school run took a few days. He felt as though he had run a marathon. The doors of Old Town Junior School finally opened, and like sand through an egg timer the assortment of children funnelled inside.

'See you on the return journey,' Anwar called out to Andrea as he push-started his bike, swinging a leg over the crossbar. *Ah, bliss*, he thought to himself. The ride home was a little bit of 'me time', when he was free of responsibilities. Shortly he'd have to climb to his studio in the top of the house. He worked as an illustrator, and however relaxed his approach to life was, a deadline was just that.

Bonzo, however, had other ideas. As Anwar slowed to cross Windmill Drive for the second time that day, Bonzo stopped to do what dogs do in the morning.

As Anwar waited, he watched a neat little van drive past. Its navy-blue paint was detailed with gold lettering, 'Wm Faulks, Est. 1884, Northcote Road', and appealed to his art-loving side.

'Nice. Less is more,' he murmured to himself. Then he screwed up his face in thought. Northcote Road was nearby. It was the main shopping street between Clapham and Battersea, pretty much the centre of the Nappy Valley world. Anwar thought he knew just about every shop on it. Admittedly the main ones that concerned the Khan family were the toy shop, the pet shop, the kids' shoe shop, Better Burgers and the Starbucks. He'd look out for Wm Faulks the next time he was there.

The little blue van was on a mission for an old client. William Faulks & Son had come into being just two years after the creation of the Ashes Urn, and the company had a long-established connection with Lord's Cricket Ground. The business had originally been located in swanky Knightsbridge. Wm Faulks: Jewellers and Silversmiths to the well-heeled. At that time cricket was run by wealthy individuals, in an era far removed from logos and sponsorship. Therefore, if Lord La-Dee-Daa or Sir Spencer Cecil Brabazon Ponsonby-Fane (that is a real name) wanted a trophy to recognise his XI then where better to go than William Faulks & Son around the corner?

As the years passed and the cost of property in the area escalated, the business relocated. Yet all these decades later, the link had remained. When Mr Bradfield was in his darkest hour of need, who should he call but the current Mr Faulks? As he passed Anwar, cutting through Clapham Common, he was on his way to St John's Wood to collect the damaged trophy.

As the vehicle disappeared into the distance, Anwar called Bonzo to him.

'Come along, Bonz, that's enough hanging around for you and me. Let's get you home before the paparazzi see you.'

Chapter 4 – The Toolbox Gang Rides Again

The jingle of an old-fashioned doorbell as the café door opened made Finn O'Toole look up. The Boiled Egg and Soldier was an unlikely venue for a meeting of two criminal masterminds.

'You found it, then.'

'Found it. Yes, obviously.' Jago rolled his eyes. 'But parking is a nightmare. What sort of damn fool idea of a place to meet is this?'

'One that's off the radar and one that does a great bacon roll. Two bacon rolls and two teas, please,' he called out to the girl behind the counter.

'It's close to the target, I'll give you that.'

The café was situated in a parade of shops on one side of Northcote Road. It was popular with young families and offered a healthy option to fast food. It not only provided excellent cover but overlooked the jewellers, William Faulks & Son.

'You've been in and cased the joint.'

'I have indeed.'

'...and?'

'Front door on a buzzer, one girl at the reception. An office in the back, curtained off from the shop, with some old geezer in it doing stuff.'

'We can't hit it during the day, not with this lot around.' He nodded in the direction of their fellow diners.

'No, after hours. In the back office there's a nice, big old black Victorian cast-iron safe. It's a beautiful thing in many ways. The main one being it'll be a doddle to crack. We'll be in and out in double-quick time. Like a robber's dog, as they say.'

'Do they, now? Well, this robber's dog likes to have a good sniff around before he pokes his snout into anywhere.'

Their conversation was brought to an abrupt halt as the waitress placed their rolls and mugs of tea on the table in front of them.

'Here you go, guys. Will there be anything else?'

Finn could see that his brother was not in the mood for chit-chat.

'Just some brown sauce, if you have it?' he cut in.

'We'll pay them another visit when we've done here, and I'll take a look for myself,' Jago started again once the girl had gone.

'Don't you think they'll be suspicious if I go in again?'

'You can put these on.' Jago retrieved a dusty pair of sunglasses from his pocket and tossed them across the table.

Finn put them on. 'How do I look?' he asked with a cheesy grin.

Across the road, inside the shop, Mr Faulks was on the telephone. He had collected the trophy without incident. Now, having had a chance to inspect the damage, he was reporting back to Mr Bradfield.

'Yes, I had a look. No, nothing too serious. I bet you nearly had kittens... Haha! Probably just a couple of days. There's a little weld I need to do, and then I'll have to polish it up.' Mr Faulks rocked his chair back on two legs and leaned back against the safe. He patted the trophy's case, propped up against it, as he delivered the news.

The Faulks' safe was a lovely old thing, painted black with gold detailing. In the late 1800s, the Milner's fire-resistant safe had been at the cutting edge of technology. Since then the lock had been changed a couple of times to satisfy the insurance company. But it was essentially the same piece of kit that the original William Faulks had used. The trophy had proved too big for it. Mr Faulks had emptied its shelves, moved things around, but could not make it fit. Well, he wouldn't draw attention to it, just set it down behind his desk and it would be fine.

The angry rasp of the shop entry phone sounded from the showroom. There was a pause, Vanessa, Mr Faulk's assistant, buzzed the customers in.

'Hello, may I help you?' She eyed the pair warily. Dealing with the public on a day-to-day basis, she had learned that people were not always as they seemed. Despite this rule of thumb, dark glasses were not a good sign, and these two looked decidedly dodgy.

'I want to get married,' Finn blurted.

'You are getting married,' Jago corrected. 'I'm sorry, miss, I'm afraid my brother is a bit overexcited at the prospect of marrying his darling Dolores.'

Finn nodded dumbly in agreement.

'Would you have any engagement rings we could have a look at?' Jago stayed in character.

'Yes, indeed. Would you mind stepping in so that I can close the door?'

The unlikely groom-to-be and his brother stepped over the threshold.

'Do you have a budget in mind? The girl asked Finn.
'Two hundr…'

'Two thousand,' Jago broke in.

'We should be able to find you something very nice for two thousand pounds.'

Vanessa took her place behind one of the glass cabinets and extracted a tray of rings from it.

'I'm happy to try anything on for you, you know, to see how they look on a woman's hand.'

As Finn played the love-struck fiancé, Jago had a surreptitious snoop around. The front door was clearly heavily alarmed. The window also had silver contact strips running through it. At the back of the shop, behind the curtain, he could see the edge of the old safe. He made his way over to have a look, and just started to push the thick velvet to one side.

'This area is private, I'm afraid.' Mr Faulks, who had been monitoring the two men, stepped forward and stopped Jago in his tracks.

'Sorry, old son, no need to get shirty. I thought there might be more stuff back here,' Jago replied, putting a restraining hand on Mr Faulks' chest.

'Unhand me, sir!' he said rather pompously.

Taking the rebuke, Jago moodily sidled over to where Finn was standing.

'Surely, you'd be better off without your sunglasses, sir?' suggested Vanessa.

'He has an eye condition, I'm afraid, so he'll be keeping them on.' Jago's tone suggested that there would be no arguing this point.

'If you don't mind, gentlemen, we are closing early today. Perhaps you could come back another day.' Mr Faulks had seen enough of these two. 'Vanessa, perhaps you'd like to go through to the office while I see the gentlemen out.'

'Oh, our money not good enough for you, is it?' Jago barked. 'Well, you can keep your rings, they look like they're made of paste anyway.'

The two men left the shop, and Mr Faulks gave them a withering look as he slid the door bolts home.

'Seen everything you need to?' Finn asked as they walked away.

'Pretty much. Let's have a snoop around the back and see if we can find some other way in. I like the look of this alleyway here, and next door is promising too. There looks to be the remains of a fire-escape ladder attached to it. That could get us onto the roof.'

While the O'Toole brothers padded around the outside of the shop the telephone rang inside.

'Bradfield here. The trophy's absence is already becoming something of a problem. It seems a newspaper wants to take its photo the day after tomorrow. Is there any way you can hurry things along and get it back to me before that?'

'Funny you should call, Bradders, I was just thinking the same thing myself,' replied a thoughtful Mr Faulks. Being in the jewellery trade, he was always conscious of an unspoken threat hanging over him, and his two visitors had spooked him considerably.

Chapter 5 – Strictly Cricket

At Old Town Junior School, the first day had started out fun and just got better. At the morning assembly, Miss How, the head teacher, had finished up the proceedings with an announcement. Later that morning they'd be having a visit from a well-known sports personality. She left it at that.

There had been lots of talk that it might be David Beckham. As unlikely as this was, the rumour had sent a buzz of excitement through the place. At the appointed time the children had traipsed back into the gym and sat expectantly on the floor. Mr Penny, the sports coach, lowered the screen from the ceiling and adjusted a microphone. He then welcomed the guest, who had been hovering in the doorway, and introduced him.

'Some of you may recognise him from *Strictly Come Dancing*, others from the cricket pitch. I'd like everyone to give an Old Town Junior School welcome, to Mr...'

'I don't recognise him,' Lita said loudly to her friend Coco.

'No, me neither.'

'What was his name?' whispered another.

'Ssh,' warned Mr Penny as he took up his seat at the side of the room.

'He's got a real England tracksuit,' Nish observed.

'I've definitely seen him on the telly.' Zak backed him up.

The guest was self-deprecating and apologised for being so old. Most of the kids hadn't been born when he'd won *Strictly*, he joked.

'Before I get started, I'm going to show you a video.' He clicked on a laptop key, and Freddie Flintoff, the face of English cricket, appeared on the screen. He was sitting at a café table reading a newspaper. On the back page were the words 'CRICKET WORLD CUP IS COMING'. No sooner had the children focused on this than he was up on his feet breaking into a version of 'On Top of The World', supported, out of nowhere, by a cast of thousands. Children, famous faces and people from all over the world were marching to the music. They processed through the streets of London to their destination, the Oval Cricket Ground. It finished with Freddie striking his famous down-on-one-knee, arms outstretched, pose. Here was cricket's messiah.

The children weren't quite sure what to make of this assault on their senses. Everyone loved the song, and the video had an upbeat, feel-good factor. But what exactly did it mean?

'Can anyone tell me who won the World Cup?' the visitor asked, pausing his laptop.

Hands shot up all around the room.

'Yes, you.'

'Easy. France,' the selected child replied.

'Hmm... What if I were to tell you it was England?'

'You'd be talking about the Women's Cricket World Cup,' called out Harry.

'Absolutely right, well done you.'

There was a sceptical murmur around the room.

'On July 2017 at Lord's Cricket Ground the England women's team beat India by just nine runs.'

'I went to the final,' Harry called out proudly.

'I'll bet you had a great time, too. Ask anyone who was at the ground that day, all twenty-four thousand of them. Everyone involved said it was an exceptional day. Quite unlike any day's cricket they had experienced before. Mainly, I guess, because it was a different crowd to the one that normally turns up at Lord's.

'The reason I'm here is to pass on the great news that next year we're doing it all over again. Ten teams from ten countries, weather permitting –' he allowed himself a smirk – 'will compete for the 2019 Men's version of the Cricket World Cup. What's more, the first match is taking place just two miles down the road from here.'

The children's collective 'HUH?' suggested that this news had passed by most of them until now.

'Just think, a global sporting event on your own doorstep. The first match takes place at the Oval Cricket Ground in Kennington on May the thirtieth, 2019. England, the hosts, take on South Africa.'

The 'HUH?' turned into an 'OOOH!'

'Let's see how many of the nations taking part are represented in this room.'

It turned out that only the Australians were not represented, Lita having made the case that their next-door neighbour counted as the New Zealand representative. Otherwise, England, South Africa, Bangladesh, Pakistan, India, Afghanistan, the West Indies and Sri Lanka would all be guaranteed at least one cheer.

'Who plays cricket here?' was the next question.

Some of the boys said that they played in the cricket nets on Clapham Common. Others admitted to a bit of garden cricket. Harry put his hand up again.

'I play for Spencer Cricket Club in Wandsworth.'

'They have an excellent set-up, lots of teams and a good link with my old team, Surrey County Cricket Club.'

Harry flushed with pride at the recognition.

The upbeat presentation was capped with a free hand-out. A press-out cardboard cricket game that everyone was pleased with.

'There's even a little trophy,' Nish cried, waving his freebie over his head.

Fired up by their introduction to the Cricket World Cup, everyone wanted to play cricket at lunch break. Mr Penny had predicted this and had sorted out some bats and practice balls.

All the activity was supported by a soundtrack of the children singing a chorus of 'I'm on top of the world, heh!'

The children were still buzzing at school pick-up time. Lita came out of the door first, pushing her bike.

'Good day, hun?' Anwar asked.

'Yes, it was chicken nuggets for lunch,' she replied simply, giving Bonzo a 'hello' stroke as if this was all school had been about.

Zak appeared and got a telling-off for giving the school doors a clonk with his bike pedal.

'Take it easy, son,' Anwar warned.

Zak ignored him. 'Hey, Dad, a real cricketer came and talked to us about the Cricket World Cup,' he announced.

'Really? How cool. Who was it?'

'I don't remember his name. But it was interesting. Can we go?'

'To the World Cup? Sure, if we can get tickets and they aren't too expensive. When is it?'

'Daaad... What do you mean you don't know when it is, you big silly billy face...?' Zak taunted his father in a sing-song way.

'Why you little...'

They'd reached the bike path, and Zak put his foot down and sped off. Lita, who liked the tone of Zak's odd put-down, was left repeatedly chanting 'silly billy face'.

'Hey, see you at the bandstand,' Anwar called after him.

Zak gave an airy wave and jagged to the right towards the Victorian bandstand. There was a café by it, and Anwar had arranged to meet a good friend and fellow illustrator there. By the time the others arrived, Zak had already met up with Rik. The kids knew him well and were fond of him. They liked his jokey nature and ready smile. Above all, he was a grown-up who didn't take himself too seriously. Zak had cycled up and rested a foot on the park bench he was sitting on. As he sat on the saddle and chatted with his father's friend, he rocked his bike to and fro.

'Look, Rik's got his ninja shoes on,' he called out to the others. They all looked at Rik's feet. He was wearing some Japanese shoes that divided his toes.

'Don't you start,' pleaded Rik. 'I took my mum to the doctor's today and a little kid shouted, "Granny, look, that ninja has come to the doctors' with his mum!"'

Anwar stifled a snort. Bonzo came to the rescue and nuzzled up against Rik for a pat.

'Thank you, Bonzo. At least someone is on my side.'

While the two men chatted, the children made circuits of the bandstand. Bonzo, who tended not to wander far away, went into full exploratory sniff mode. His snout was perfectly shaped for the job. It just cleared the ground, while providing an excellent angle of sniff for his black wine-gum of a nose.

'DAAD-DY!' is a cry that sends a shiver through any parent. When Anwar heard Lita's panicked cry, he was on his feet and running in an instant. Paths fanned out in the shape of a star from the bandstand, and Anwar sprinted down the one that led in the direction of the shout. He found both the children on the grass by the duck pond. Bonzo lay between them, his paws clamped either side of his snout.

'Is everyone okay?' Anwar burst out breathlessly.

'Bonzo's hurt himself,' Lita wailed.

'He was rummaging about in the reeds by the pond. Suddenly he let out a yelp and came running over to us. He's been rubbing his nose on the grass and whimpering,' Zak explained.

'Let's have a look at you, fella,' Anwar said soothingly, holding Bonzo's paws away from his snout. 'Hmm, nothing I can see, but clearly he's not happy.'

'Perhaps he's been stung by a wasp,' Rik, who had joined them, suggested.

'That's a good call,' Anwar replied. 'His nose seems to be swelling up a bit. I guess we'd better take him to the vet. Come on, kids, get your bikes.'

'Where do you take him?' asked Rik.

'To Mr Bumby's clinic, near Balham Tube station.'

'I'll take him for you,' Rik offered. 'You've got the kids and your bikes. We can just hop on the bus, Bonzo and I.'

'Really? That would be a lifesaver, Rik.'

'No worries. You'll come with me, won't you, Bonzo?' The little dog allowed himself to be scooped up without protest. 'I'll text you when I have some news,' Rik called over his shoulder.

'He'll be all right, won't he, Daddy?' Lita looked a bit teary. 'Of course. Now let's get home and make his bed all nice for him for when he gets back.'

The text from Rik arrived in due course, and the news was cautiously optimistic.

'The Doc says B is okay, but he wants to keep him for a couple of hours in case he has had a reaction to something. I am happy to wait.'

'Rik, u r a saint,' Anwar replied.

Rik appeared at six o'clock with a much perkier-looking Bonzo.

'Dude, what can I say?' Anwar cried. 'I can't believe you had to wait so long.'

Rik pulled a face like the clenched-teeth emoji.

'It was fine.' He made a comedy gulping sound, as though he was choking back tears.

'I owe you one, my friend.' Anwar clapped him on the back. 'Bonzo does too.'

Chapter 6 – Northcote Night

That evening there was a splash of rain, the first for some time. On Northcote Road, the street lights were mirrored in the sheen on the tarmac. An office worker, late home from work, hurried down the street. The side roads that branched off this main shopping street were a warren of terraced houses. The man turned left and disappeared to the sanctuary of one of them.

A silver, mini-van-sized people carrier was parked up in a shadowy parking space, its rain-spotted windows partly obscuring the three figures hunched inside. The atmosphere between them was what might be called tense. While they patiently kept a lookout on their intended target, the Toolbox Gang was experiencing a personnel issue.

'You cannot be serious,' Jago hissed through the darkness.

'It was last-minute, what else could I do?'

Muppet looked shiftily in the mirror of the recently acquired people carrier. Two heavy-set silhouettes were remonstrating with each other behind him. The vehicle bounced on its springs as the pair argued vigorously.

'I told you...'

'...and I got it sorted,' Finn finished his brother's sentence.

'This is the second job in a row you've messed up.' Jago jabbed Muppet in the shoulder. Muppet tensed but decided it was probably best not to get any deeper involved in the argument. He flicked on the windscreen wipers and watched them sweep the rain away.

'He's in on it now, and we've come too far,' Finn concluded. 'That's an end to it. We have a living to make and our reputation to keep up. We're not pulling out of another job. If we go on like this, the only thing we're going to be known for is for being the most law-abiding crooks in South London. We'll be a laughing stock.'

'Seeing as you put it like that,' as Jago rubbed his chin thoughtfully, a chunky gold bracelet slipped down his wrist with a jingle. 'This is it, though, I don't want to see this little twerp again –' apparently meaning Muppet – 'after tonight.'

They settled down and went into stealth mode. The gang was just waiting for one last nearby restaurant to finish serving. At last, the lights flicked off as the staff closed up for the night. In the darkness the mini-van blended into the street furniture as anonymously as all the other parked vehicles. Finn and Jago both pulled on balaclavas and gave the inhabitants of Northcote Road ten more minutes to settle. Then, with a nod to each other, the operation began. Finn silently slid the side door off the van and Jago stepped out.

'You, keep your eyes peeled and watch for our signal,' Jago ordered Muppet as he heaved a canvas bag from the van's floor. The tools inside it clanked, and he placed a hand under it to deaden the sound.

'He's a pussycat, really,' Finn said conspiratorially to Muppet, as he stepped out to join his brother.

Now they moved quickly and decisively. Checking that the coast was clear, the brothers sprinted across the road. They were light on their feet as well as with their fingers. Ducking into the shadows, they lingered for a moment in front of William Faulks, the jewellers. A wooden gate had been fastened across the entrance to the doorway and the shop had been left in complete darkness. Jago pressed his face up against the plate-glass window and saw a little red light piercing the darkness.

'Burglar alarm armed, control box located,' he whispered to his accomplice. 'I was pretty sure we'd be able to go straight through the front door, but I think we'll have a little look at the back.'

'Down here,' Finn hissed, and the pair ducked down the little alleyway to the right of the shop. As soon as they'd disappeared into it, there was a nerve-jangling sound of breaking glass. Jago had kicked and smashed a discarded empty beer bottle. The noise prompted a theatrical hiss from a cat that was doing its rounds.

The two figures pressed themselves flat against the damp brickwork of the building and waited again. Content that they had yet to be detected, they pressed on. The alleyway was a dead end. A whitewashed brick wall looked as though it would give access to the back of the building. It wasn't too high and was easily climbable.

'Give me a bunk up, will ya?' said Finn. Jago put the bag down with a clank and linked his fingers to form a step for his brother. Finn leaped up with a well-practised spring, and Jago assisted.

No sooner had Finn launched himself then he let out an ear-splitting yelp. The top of the wall had a strip of plastic spikes set into the top as a deterrent. Finn had tried to pull his weight up by planting both his hands firmly on it.

He skidded back down the wall, further scraping his chin. He whimpered pitifully as he jammed his hands under his armpits to soothe them.

'Do you think you could keep the noise down?' Jago snapped. As he spoke, his eyes lighted upon a much more straightforward way into the building – the rusty black wrought-iron fire-escape ladder bolted to the wall. They'd missed it in the dark.

The ladder had seen better days and was missing a few rungs. *But we can handle that, right?* Jago thought to himself. *If Finn gets his act together, then hell yeah.*

Not wanting to take any further chances Jago decided to take the lead. He weighed the tool bag in his hand before grasping a rung of the ladder. It felt good and firm, and he started to climb. Finn kept a lookout as his brother disappeared skywards and then out of view. In no time his silhouette appeared over the edge of the roof.

'Psst...!' He urged Finn to join him, and in no time the two were on top of the shop.

'Would you look at that? A nice rotten skylight.' Jago allowed himself the faintest glimmer of a smile beneath his woolly mask. The moon provided just enough light for them to size up the white-painted wooden frame. Jago pushed a finger into a dark patch. The wood was saturated and rotten and gave under the pressure.

'Beautiful,' Jago cooed. Together the men prised open the skylight. Jago secured it and lowered himself through the frame.

'There's a little attic space,' he murmured to Finn. There wasn't sufficient room for them to stand but they managed to cram themselves in there anyway. Jago switched on a thin torch.

Flashing it around them, they could see that the some of the attic had been fitted with boards screwed to the joists. Dusty cardboard boxes were stacked neatly on top of them. A square empty space in the middle of the attic suggested the way down to the shop.

'Voila,' said Jago, picking it out with the torch beam. 'Just make sure to stick to the boarded areas.'

They edged around the space until they were crouched either side of the attic trapdoor. With the torch clamped between his teeth, Jago eased it up and pushed it back on its hinge. A shower of dust fell to the floor below. As it settled, three short *BEEP* sounds followed by a longer one sounded in the darkness. Jago reached out in panic to close the attic door. He failed to grasp it, lost his balance and plunged through the hole.

In response, Finn reeled backwards and put his foot between two of the exposed joists. It went straight through the thin plaster ceiling, sending a further shower of dust and fragments through the room below.

Jago's cry and the thump of his landing on the floor below had been mainly drowned out by Finn's efforts. Now the clattering of the various tools as they scattered themselves about him brought the cacophony to a crescendo.

'Are you all right down there?' Finn asked once everything had settled.

A single, doleful groan floated up to him.

'I'll be right with you, old son, don't you worry,' he called down in an attempt to calm his brother. Finn managed to extricate himself from the ceiling with a couple of good hard yanks. He then lowered himself to what turned out to be a small landing with a banister on one side and a set of stairs leading down from it. In horror, he realised that Jago had bypassed this design feature. It seemed he had fallen from the roof to the ground floor in one fell swoop. It was no wonder he was groaning.

It had not taken long for the Alarm Receiving Centre, to contact the Lavender Hill Police Station. However, the fact that the alarm wasn't connected directly to the police did buy the gang some time, although they were not aware of it. Finn tore down the stairs, turned on a light and fell to his knees beside his brother.

'Jago, are you still with us?'

'Get me out of here,' he croaked.

Finn glanced about the shop. The front door was firmly locked and bolted. Escape that way seemed impossible. He ducked into a little kitchenette and found that there was a door in the back wall. It had to lead to the alley. Two bolts, top, and bottom, secured it. He slid them both open and wrenched the handle. The door wouldn't budge as it was locked with a key. There was nothing else for it. In his panic, he put one foot up against the frame and gave it a superhuman pull. The lock gave way, and the door flew open. The light spilling into the alleyway caught Muppet's attention, and he wasn't surprised when he saw Finn out in front of the shop gesticulating to him wildly.

'Get, over here I need your help,' he hissed.

Muppet undid his seat belt and hopped out of the van.

'Jago's had a fall, he doesn't look too good. I think we'll have to carry him. Quick, come with me.'

Muppet hesitated. He wasn't keen on visiting the scene of the crime. However, if Jago was really hurt, perhaps he should.

On one side of Wandsworth Common, a police patrol car was just getting the news of an alarm being triggered.

'Suspected break-in attempt at Faulks Jewellers, Northcote Road.'

'Ten-four, message received. We'll nip down and take a look.' The driver peeled off the main road and down one of the side streets. The Victorians had not planned on there being a car parked outside every house, on both sides of the road, so for the police driver progress had to be made with caution. There was only one useable lane, down the middle. Add to that the road humps every fifty metres. Consequently, the police car's progress was, not to put too fine a point on it, slow.

Back inside the shop, Jago had started to pick himself up.

'Go on, give him your shoulder,' Finn ordered Muppet.

Muppet did as he was told and together he and the big man limped out through the kitchenette.

'Finn, get that little trinket box on top of the safe,' Jago barked, pointing out a small, locked, metal cabinet. 'I'm not going through all this for nothing.' He grimaced with pain.

Finn did as he was told. He stood in front of the big old safe for a moment and gave it a wistful stroke, but time was against them, and he knew better than to cross Jago. He picked up the little cabinet and put it under his arm. As he turned around, he spotted the silver aluminium suitcase that had been picked up from Mr Bradfield. 'Might as well have you too, my beauty,' he said under his breath.

The case was big and cumbersome. It banged on the walls of the narrow alley as he followed the other two out. Jago and Muppet were just crossing the road.

'What the dickens is that?'

'The box you wanted.'

'No, the other thing, you mug. Ditch it,' Jago ordered.

Muppet and Finn manhandled Jago in through the side door of the mini-van. He slumped on the middle set of seats with a groan. Finn picked up the little cabinet and put it on the floor behind him. Just as he was about to hop into the van, he paused. *What harm could it do?* he thought. He shunted the case in and followed it, sliding the door home with a bang.

'Hit it!' Jago cried, and Muppet gunned the engine. He pulled away just as the police car arrived, and the two vehicles passed each other without incident.

'See that?' the constable in the passenger seat asked the driver.

'No lights.'

The driver executed a three-point turn and his colleague gave the blue light a flash.

In the van, Finn looked over his shoulder.

'The Fuzz, they're onto us!' he cried.

Without consultation, Muppet pulled a sharp left turn and floored the accelerator. The van entered a side street lined with parked cars and bounded over the first hump. Finn and Jago let out a mixed cry of 'WHOA!' and 'YEE-OUCH!'

The bumps aren't called sleeping policemen for nothing, Muppet thought, as the inanimate bumps slowed their progress. Behind them, a blue light showed the police car had entered the street.

This maze of roads was an irregular grid pattern, but Muppet knew it well. He made a sharp right at the top of the road, took a short straight section, then left again. He worked hard on the wheel, sawing this way and that, taking the humps with a touch of the brakes and then hard back down on the accelerator. All the time his passengers were being bounced around the interior of the van.

They had now turned back on themselves. The road names flashed by: Chatto, right onto Webb's, a left turn and down a steep hill on Chatham. Suddenly Muppet pulled on the handbrake and turned the wheel hard left. The mini-van slewed round in a neat arc and Muppet turned down a dead end. Immediately he stopped and killed the engine. They waited in the dark silence, all of them breathless, and the mini-van wheezing slightly. Behind them the police car flashed by, having missed them.

'He's a genius,' Finn said warmly.

'Not yet, he isn't,' Jago countered harshly, as lights started to come on in the upstairs windows of the houses. Before anyone could challenge them, Muppet backed the mini-van back onto the main road. He threaded a path through the little streets and soon they were out of the residential area and able to blend into the night-time London traffic.

'We've got to ditch this motor,' Jago barked as they drove around the south side of Clapham Common.

'Have you got another car parked up to make a switch?' Muppet cried, a hint of desperation in his voice.

'In case you haven't noticed, the Toolbox Gang is a bit light on personnel at the moment, and don't think you're getting paid...' Jago didn't finish the sentence. The full beam of the police car's headlights lit up the inside of the van. The police had parked up in the council's access road to the football pitches on the common.

'GO, GO, GO!' urged Finn. Muppet didn't need telling twice, and he jabbed his foot hard down on the accelerator.

This time the police had the jump on them, and were in close pursuit. Muppet was either going to have to tear up the Highway Code and do something incredibly reckless, or go off road. Which he did!

He gave the wheel a sharp twitch, and the van bumped up the curb. Once again, the occupants tumbled around the interior. The suitcase slithered across the floor and banged into Jago's damaged leg. He let out a blood-curdling scream.

'I told you to dump that!' He swivelled in his seat and spat the words at Finn.

The mini-van sideswiped one of the common's perimeter fence posts. There was a hideous sound of metal being gouged then the fence gave way, and the vehicle lurched onto the main island of the common.

'This thing is going,' Jago bellowed over the din. He reached over and grabbed the side door, and as he slid it open he pushed out the suitcase. He slammed the door shut with a triumphant roar.

The suitcase hit the ground, its metal edge striking a flinty spark. Its momentum sent it spinning end over end, and it bounced as it struck a patch of asphalt. Meanwhile, with their unexpected access to an otherwise completely off-limits area of London, the gang made good their escape. Muppet ploughed across the common, skirted the boating lake and disappeared through Clapham Old Town.

Throughout the chase, the police car's radio had crackled. The Lambeth stations had been alerted to the situation and the police officers had called off their pursuit. They had the public's safety to take into consideration and had come to a stop in Windmill Lane. The Chuck Wagon, re-opened for business, and at all hours too, provided a tempting pit-stop. The two men got out of their car, stretched, and wandered over to the wagon.

As they searched the menu a loud honking sounded from the nearby pond.

'We've done it now, we've upset the neighbours,' one of the officers joked.

He was right, too. A large female Canada goose was pecking aggressively at the large item that had lodged itself in her nest. Embedded in the reeds lay the Cricket World Cup, safely contained in its case.

Chapter 7 – A Star is Reborn

Mr Faulks' telephone rang, and he reached for it on the nightstand.

'Mr Faulks? I'm sorry to disturb you in the middle of the night. I'm calling from Battersea Police Station. Sergeant Tennant on the line.'

'Hullo,' Mr Faulks replied groggily.

'I'm calling with bad news, I'm afraid. I realise that this isn't the best way to be woken up, but you've had a break-in at your shop. We'd really like you to come down and help identify anything that's missing. You'll want to make the premises secure in any case.'

Mr Faulks put the phone handset on the bed beside him and rubbed his face with the palms of his hands.

'Mr Faulks? Err, Mr Faulks?' Sergeant Tennant's voice squeaked from it.

Having regained his composure, Mr Faulks picked up the receiver.

'I'll be right there.' Now his voice was measured, unflappable.

Apart from the damage to the skylight, the ceiling and the back door, the shop was remarkably unscathed. The locked chest of drawers had gone but it had contained only low-value items. Anything of any worth was still safely locked away in the safe.

'At least the alarm system proved effective,' Mr Faulks murmured.

Sergeant Tennant was finding it hard to take him seriously. He'd had to dress quickly, and stuffed his bare feet into stout shoes and pulled an overcoat over his striped pyjamas.

'Yes, indeed,' the policeman agreed. 'We'll need to reset that and dust for fingerprints.'

Two guys from a 24-hour call-out burglary-repair company were hard at work making the shop secure. Mr Faulks tried to make himself heard over their banging.

'There is something else that's missing. A metal suitcase.'

'Yes, we'll be on the case,' Tennant replied, cupping a hand to one ear.

'No, I've lost a case. It really is of the utmost importance that we get it back.' Mr Faulks explained about the case and its contents.

'Oh, I see.' Tennant gave an involuntary shudder. 'That is quite awkward.'

'To say the very least! And the last thing we want is for the press to get wind of it. They will have a field day. I can see it now, the "Cricket Administrators lose cup before we get a chance to win it" headline.'

'Don't worry, I'll be the soul of discretion.' Tennant tapped the side of his nose with his finger. 'We will have to break the news eventually, though.'

'There are people I'll need to speak to first to see just how we handle that. You know what big organisations are like. Press officers, the "official line".' He drew two imaginary inverted commas in the air.

Mr Faulks returned home and got a couple more hours of sleep. The morning dawned all too quickly, and he ate his breakfast with one eye on the clock, steeling himself for the call he'd have to make to Mr Bradfield.

****

On the other side of Clapham Common, the Khan family were going through their morning routine, which was slightly altered today as Jen was working from home. Depending on who you asked, this could be viewed as either a help or a hindrance. Usually she'd have left early, stylishly turned out, polished, professional and ready to get to grips with her office job in Central London. Today she'd piled her long brown hair in an unruly mound and donned her ripped jeans, trainers and hoody. Having checked her emails, she was now free to join the rest of the family on the school run. She was looking forward to catching up with some of the other mums, having a coffee with her hubby and taking Bonzo for his walk.

'Can we just go?' Anwar said as he stood at the front door, sounding frustrated. 'Do you really need a bag?'

'I need my phone, a notebook, something to write with. You know, I'm working from home, remember?'

Bonzo was starting to lose it too, with frustration at not being let out yet.

'Bonzo! Calm down,' Zak scolded.

'Don't be horrible to Bonny,' Lita countered.

'LOOK! Would everyone just calm down,' Anwar half-shouted, making himself look foolish.

'Come along, Bonzo, let's go,' Jen announced, reaching between the others and opening the front door.

The family spilled onto the street. As they sorted out bags, the children's bicycles and the dog, their squabbles were forgotten.

Suddenly Loud Dunc rushed out of his house.

'Crikey, I overslept. Morning, all!' he bellowed before sprinting off down the street. The Khans followed him at a more sedate pace, dictated mainly by Bonzo and his need to sniff every centimetre of the street. Soon they were all crossing the common, the children cycling on ahead.

****

Across town, Mr Bradfield had arrived early for work. He liked to pick up a coffee and a croissant before settling down to read the paper for half an hour. This morning, however, his 'me' time had to be put on hold. The receptionist handed him a note with a message to give Mr Faulks a call as soon as possible. He did so from his desk in the library at Lord's Cricket Ground.

'Morning, Mr Faulks, what can I do for you?'

'Ah, Mr Bradfield, yes. Thank you for calling me back. I, err... Well, you see...'

'Come on man, spit it out.'

'The World Cup, sir.'

'Yes?'

'It's gone.'

'What on earth do you mean, gone? I handed it to you myself just the other day.'

'Yes, indeed and I've been taking great care of it. That is until last night.'

'Last night?

'Yes, I'm afraid my shop was broken into, and the World Cup has been taken.'

'WHAT!? There must be some mistake.'

'No mistake, I'm afraid. Nothing else of any real value was taken. It's almost as if someone knew it was there.'

'Good grief, what am I going to do?' Mr Bradfield said it more to himself than to Mr Faulks.

'I've given the police your details. I'm sure they'll be in touch later in the morning.'

'Oh, do you think so?' said Mr Bradfield sarcastically. 'That's a surprise.'

'I'm sorry to be the bearer of such bad news. Perhaps I should let you get on. I'm sure you have a lot to do and to think about.'

'You've not heard the end of this, Faulks,' Bradfield replied abruptly before ending the call.
What had started out as an exciting week had turned into a disaster. Mr Bradfield put his elbows on his desk and massaged his temples. He needed to think, to formulate a plan. The organisers of the World Cup competition would need to be informed. The media would need to be told, as keeping this sort of thing a secret would be bound to backfire. Finally, he would need to liaise with the police.

He made two calls in quick succession. One to Sheena O'Shea, the organisers' director of communications, and the other to the managing director of the World Cup, the unlikely named Pete Peters. A meeting was scheduled for nine o'clock in their offices on the other side of the ground. No sooner had he made these calls than the police rang him.

'Is that Mr Bradfield? Good morning, I'm sorry to call so early. I'm Detective Constable Palmer, I'm in charge of the Faulks' jewellers robbery investigation.'

'Morning. I've been expecting your call.'

'I understand that an item of yours was taken from the premises.'

'That's not strictly true. An item that I'm responsible for was taken, yes.'

There followed a drawn-out conversation about the dimensions of the cup and the case, its value, who actually owned it, and whether it was insured.

'Is there a replica?' DC Palmer asked.

A replica – now that was a thought that hadn't occurred to Mr Bradfield. Of course, there had to be a replica, if you thought about the number of miles that one trophy had to travel for press appearances in different countries. For a moment Mr Bradfield felt a considerable weight lift from his shoulders. In a worst-case scenario, they'd have a replica 2019 World Cup. It didn't have quite such a good ring to it, but, if they were in a tight spot, it would do.

'I don't have that information to hand at the moment, I'll try to get answers to any questions you have that might help the investigation.'

'Given the particular nature of the item that has been taken, it may have been stolen to order.'

'I think that is very unlikely, Detective. Only Mr Faulks and I knew that the cup was there.'

'Hmmm, that is very helpful,' DC Palmer murmured as he noted this fact down. 'At the moment,' he continued, 'we're investigating the incident along the lines of a conventional burglary. Tools that we found at the premises are undergoing forensic investigation. We're hoping that there will be fingerprint evidence that we can link to other crimes in the area.'

'Splendid, that all sounds very hopeful. I'm meeting in a moment to discuss how we release this information to the media.'

Righto, sir. I'll be in touch if I have any further questions or news for you.'

Mr Bradfield rang off and made his way to his meeting.

****

Anwar and Jen dropped the children safely at school and wandered across the common arm in arm.

'This is nice,' she said, cosying up to him.

Bonzo ran ahead, happy not to stray too far.

'For goodness' sake.' Anwar suddenly panicked. 'The dog's back in those reeds again.'

'What reeds?' Jen called after him, puzzled.

But Anwar wasn't listening. He was too intent on stopping Bonzo. Whatever had stung him in the reeds the other day might do it again. One lengthy and costly visit to the vet in a week was enough.

Anwar arrived to find Bonzo's rear protruding from the reeds. Evidently whatever was in there was incredibly interesting as the little dog was energetically rummaging about.

'Will you come out of there?' Anwar ordered, wading in and parting the reeds with his arms. To his amazement, what Bonzo had found was neither flora nor fauna. It was a honking great metal box, dented and muddied in the murky water at the edge of the pond.

'Come over here, Bonz.' Anwar pulled Bonzo out of the reeds and then stepped back in to retrieve the aluminium case.

'What have you got there?' Jen asked as she arrived and clipped Bonzo onto his lead.

'I'm not sure. It's amazing what people will dump.' Anwar held out the bashed-up case for her to inspect.

'It's terrible,' Jen agreed.

'We can't just leave it, can we? I guess we'll carry it home and I'll take it to the dump next time I'm going.'

'Perhaps they'll take it.' Jen pointed to the dustcart that was parked up by the nearby Chuck Wagon. The dustmen were tucking into their burgers in front of it.

'Excuse me, will you boys take this?' Anwar asked, walking towards them holding up the case.

'Nah, mate, we're on our lunch break,' said one.

'Don't worry, I'll just toss it into the back of your truck.'

'Just toss it in the back of our truck,' another mimicked in mock astonishment. 'You can't do that. You need to be a trained refuse disposal operative.'

'Er, okay.' Anwar shrugged. 'Better take it home, then.'

The three of them continued back to the house. The long rectangular case was awkward to walk with, and Anwar was glad to put it down. He'd bashed his leg with it a number of times and messed up his jeans.

'It's pretty heavy,' he said to Jen, and made to lay it on the counter in the kitchen.

'Wait, let me get some newspaper or something to put it on.'

Anwar rolled his eyes but waited until Jen had spread some kitchen towel out. Then he hauled it up onto the counter.

'It's really quite a heavy old thing.'

'There must be something in it, then. Have a look.'

Anwar clicked open the catches and lifted the lid.

'Oh... my... goodness,' he said deliberately.

Jen wandered up behind him and cast an absent-minded look over his shoulder at the contents.

'What on earth is it?'

Anwar hoisted the eleven-kilogram trophy from its case with difficulty. The globe at the top made it awkward to handle. He examined the engraved plates on its base for a clue.

'Australia 2015, India 2011, Australia 2007, Australia 2003, Australia 1999,' he read. 'If I had to make a guess, I would say that this is a trophy that Australia has won many times and India once,' he said jokily.

Jen leaned over and confirmed this for herself.

'Like duh, it says what it is on the top.' Jen ran her finger along the silver band encasing the gold globe at the top of the trophy. 'The GCB Cricket World Cup,' she read.

'Well, I never,' said Anwar giving his tousled black hair a rub.

****

A meeting had been hastily convened in the offices of the World Cup Competition organisers. These were on the other side of

Lord's Cricket Ground by the Indoor Cricket School. In attendance were Pete Peters, Sheena O'Shea and Mr Bradfield.

Pete Peters, always meticulous in appearance, might have been described as uptight at the best of times. His jutting jaw and pomaded hair, parted with razor-like precision, gave him a slightly sinister air. You were never entirely sure if he was with you or against you.

In contrast, Sheena was bright, breezy and confident. Always smart but just a little bit dishevelled. The roots of her blond hair betrayed just the tiniest line of black. It suggested she didn't waste her time on trivial things.

'STOLEN! You're kidding, right?' she started.

'No. I mean, yes, I'm afraid so,' Mr Bradfield looked at his shoes.

'This is a potential Public Relations disaster,' Pete Peters wailed.

There was a moment of horrible silence. Pete wrung his hands together in desperation. Sheena, however, rubbed her chin while she worked through the problem in her mind.

'Not if we handle it right. It could be a stroke of luck,' Sheena sought to calm his nerves.

'All right, I'm listening. Hit me with it.'

'It gets the Cricket World Cup into the public domain,' Sheena suggested. 'People who haven't had it on their radar before will suddenly be aware of it. Then we've got the "plucky Brits against the world" angle.' Sheena drew an imaginary banner in the air. 'We've got the World Cup on our doorstep, and what do you know? We've only gone and lost the cup. But are we downhearted? No!'

'Huh?' Pete was struggling.

'We'll beat this.' Sheena drove her fist into her palm. 'And we'll get the public to help us.'

Pete Peters' features softened from blind panic to slightly milder terror. Perhaps there was something in this crazy idea.

'Okay, but first we need to break the news. How do we do that?'

'I'll give Joe Wilson at the Beeb a call.'

'Okay, Sheena. Get on it, and don't let me down.'

****

After their discovery, Jen and Anwar had gone to separate parts of the house to complete their morning work assignments. When they met in the kitchen for lunch, the case was still where they'd left it.

'We'd better give someone a call about that after lunch, don't you think?' said Jen, pointing at the suitcase.

'I've had a look online and scoured the official website. There's no way to contact the GCB through that, but they have got a Twitter and Instagram handle. I'll send them a picture of it after lunch.'

'Okay. Shall we watch the lunchtime news?'

Jen clicked on the TV, and the two of them started to assemble their lunch. For Anwar, stuck at home, the news was a little treat. A chance to see what was going on in the world that day beyond their four walls in Clapham. Today Brexit was the first item. It seemed to have been so for weeks.

Towards the end of the news, an item caught their interest.

'We're just going over to Lord's Cricket Ground, where our sports editor, Joe Wilson, has some breaking news.'

The news broadcast cut to the reporter standing outside some gates.

'Breaking news today regarding something of a crisis in the cricket world. With just nine months to go before the World Cup, the organisers have a problem on their hands. It seems that the cup itself, the trophy here on loan to promote the competition, has been stolen.'

A small photo of the trophy popped up in the top right hand corner of the screen.

'At the moment details are sketchy. First reports suggest that it was stolen from a South London address. Police have started preliminary investigations, and we'll keep you updated as the story develops.'

The image cut back to the studio and the news anchor, who raised an eyebrow at the camera.

'Well, there's no doubt what she makes of that little fiasco,' Jen chuckled.

Anwar didn't answer. He had gone back over to the case and clicked it open.

'We've got it.' His voice was a mixture of concern and disbelief.

'How amazing is that?' Jen was far more upbeat.

'I wonder how it got on the common though?'

'I'm sure that will come out in due course. The simple fact is, that it did and we found it. Now we have to tell someone about it!'

'Yeah, sure,' Anwar said, processing the information. 'I guess we need to give someone a ring.' He grabbed his phone and started searching for an appropriate number. He typed in 'Lords Cricket Ground', which produced a telephone number. Anwar dialled it without hesitating.

'Main switchboard. How may I direct your call?' the receptionist delivered the greeting in a well-practised sing-song tone.

'Hi, yeah, err... I'm not quite sure who I should speak to regarding the missing cup.'

'Oh yes?' the girl changed her tone abruptly, suggesting that she didn't take too kindly to prank calls.

'No, I've found it. That is to say that my dog found it, but I've got it.'

'One moment, sir,' Anwar was put on hold while his call was redirected.

In his office, Mr Bradfield answered the call and listened to what the girl had to say. It sounded too good to be true. The trophy had only been stolen a matter of hours ago. 'Would you just ask the gentleman to hold for a moment?'

Mr Bradfield called DC Palmer on his mobile phone and told him the news.

'Take the call and put in on speaker for me to listen in,' Palmer directed.

Mr Bradfield did as he was told and asked for Anwar to be put through.

Anwar introduced himself and continued.

'My wife and I were on the school run. We'd dropped the children off and were just giving the dog a bit of a run on Clapham Common. The dog was having a snuffle around, as they do, and the next thing we know he's found this dirty great big metal case. We thought it had just been chucked away by someone. It wasn't until we saw the news that we knew what we had.'

'Really?' There was doubt in Mr Bradfield's tone. 'Are you able to describe exactly what you've found?'

'Yes, a metal case just under a metre long. Then inside it is a cup, a trophy, call it what you will. It's made up of three silver columns on a base with a golden globe on the top. There's a silver band engraved with the words *GCB Cricket World Cup* round it. It is pretty unmistakable.'

'That is extraordinary,' Mr Bradfield, now unofficially the most relieved man in the world, gushed. 'I'm sorry to have sounded so sceptical but I'm sure you understand why I had to be cautious. Your call came out of the blue, and I must say it has brightened up what was a bleak morning. Let me take down your address, we'll send a car to you.'

Anwar spelled out his address and assured him that someone would be in for the rest of the day. They said their goodbyes and Mr Bradfield picked up his mobile phone.

'Well, I never,' said DC Palmer. 'Sounds like you've dodged a bullet, you jammy stinker. I think perhaps it would be wiser to send a squad car to pick it up, no?'

Mr Bradfield wasn't sure that the 'jammy stinker' tag was entirely necessary, but he did have to admit that things had worked out better than he could have hoped. Now he had to reverse the wheels he had put into motion earlier in the day.

Questions would be asked, and he wasn't out of the woods by any means yet. The whole matter of security would have to be addressed. Mr Bradfield would have to admit that he had breached the guidelines laid out by the guardians of the cup spectacularly. Namely, not to part with it under any circumstances to anybody. In the meantime, he was keen to pass on the good news.

Pete Peters and Sheena O'Shea were in his office in a flash.

'Found by a dog?' Pete's patience had been severely tested during the course of the day, and this was a step too far.

'Yes, a dog.'

'How fantastic is that?' Sheena enthused. 'Not only are we out of the woods but now we have a great news story to spin.'

'I like your thinking, Sheena.' Pete perked up. 'You'll issue an updated press release.'

'Leave it to me.'

****

For the second time that day Joe Wilson found himself framed by the gates of Lord's Cricket Ground.

'We're going live to the studio in three, two, one...' He was counted in by the sound recordist.

'In a chaotic day of news, a story that we brought you at lunchtime has come full circle. Earlier today the organisers of next year's Cricket World Cup had to make the embarrassing admission that they had lost the trophy. It was stolen while undergoing a secret repair to damage it sustained in their care.'

Laid out in such stark terms the report was an uncomfortable watch for anyone involved.

'However, by tea time not only has the trophy been found but it appears we have an unlikely hero in a dog called Bonzo. It is a story reminiscent of that of Pickles, the dog who found the Football World Cup in 1966. That trophy had been stolen on purpose. On this occasion, it seems the cricket trophy was mistakenly taken and then dumped on Clapham Common. It was here that Bonzo, a three-year-old black and white cockapoo, made his find. As yet Bonzo has been unavailable for comment. A spokesman for him said he would *paws* and reflect *fur* a while on his new celebrity status.'

The news anchor groaned as the reporter handed back to the studio. There was, however, some truth in the description of Bonzo as a celebrity. The media coverage was only getting started.

Chapter 8 – I'm a Celebrity... Get Me Out of Here!

The next morning the family were startled by the announcement of Bonzo's celebrity on breakfast television.

'Those of you who have been following the story will already know of Bonzo, the dog who has dug the organisers of the Cricket World Cup out of a hole by finding the – accidentally, it says here –' he pointed to the autocue, '– stolen trophy. I'm not quite sure how anything gets stolen accidentally,' he said with a smirk to his fellow presenter. His colleague nodded wisely to confirm this observation, as they sat like Tweedledum and Tweedledee before the camera.

'But it seems that this isn't the first time Bonzo has been the focus of media attention. Earlier in the year, he alerted a local tradesman to a fire.'

'No!' The other presenter expressed mock disbelief.

'Yes, it seems Bonzo is some sort of "wonder dog".' He let the name hang in the air a moment. Bonzo the Wonder Dog was a label that would stick. The presenter pressed his earpiece into his ear as the Director fed him information. 'I've just been told that we're hoping to have the little chap here on the sofa tomorrow,' he said brightly.

The presenter's jaunty disposition was just a little irritating for the time of the morning, Anwar thought. He poured cereal into two bowls and set them down in front of Zak and Lita who had joined him. Also, who said that Bonzo was going to appear on breakfast television? Perhaps it was in one of those emails he'd ignored. There had been so many.

'Is Bonzo going to be on TV, Dad?' asked Zak.

'May I be on TV too?' Lita chipped in.

'No, I mean I don't know. We'll see. Eat your breakfast.'

****

Down the road, in the Balham Café, Jago and Finn were having breakfast. The two of them had spent the night at the local hospital. Now Jago was wearing a plastic boot and walking tentatively with a pronounced limp. They were both hurting from the realisation of what they had let slip through their fingers.

The delivery of early-morning newspapers to the hospital had confirmed that they had made the news. They had read that not only had they stolen the trophy but they had managed to chuck it away. Also, the police were following several leads and analysing CCTV footage. The brothers would have to watch themselves. Clearly it wouldn't be long before the police were paying them a visit.

A television suspended from a jointed arm was showing the breakfast show. The words 'wonder dog' had just registered with Finn.

'Now, I could do with a wonder dog like that.'

'Aah, you're soft in the head. There's no such thing as a wonder dog.'

'Sure there is, they're telling us all about him, and what's more he's going to be on the telly tomorrow.'

'Perhaps you're right.' Jago rubbed the stubble on his chin. 'Where is it they film that breakfast telly programme?' He pointed at the screen.

'I don't know, but we could find out,' Finn replied brightly.

'We're going to have to lie low for a bit. I'm thinking if we're going into hiding then we could take the little fella with us. I should think that people would pay a handsome price for the return of a wonder dog.' He spoke these last words in a sort of mystical tone.

****

Dolly and Tushar had already picked up on the 'wonder dog' angle in their shop just one station down the Tube line. Several papers had covered the story too and used a photo of Bonzo that had been lifted from Anwar's Facebook page.

Dolly and Tushar had been hard at work sorting out papers for delivery for some time. Now that the rush hour was in full swing they were doing a brisk trade. Tushar was standing at the door regulating the number of children allowed in the shop at any one time.

'You'll want to get a copy of today's paper, there's a local story in it,' he said, always keen to make a sale.

'What, this little dog in the picture?' a man asked, holding a newspaper open to the page of the article.

'Yeah, he's in our shop all the time. He'll be along in a minute,' Dolly added.

'There he is, look!' Tushar pointed at the little party on their way to school.

The Khan family passed by the window: Anwar, Zak and Lita with Bonzo in tow.

'Hey, Anwar!' Tushar called through the open shop door.

'Come on, kids, let's keep going,' Anwar chivvied the kids along. 'I'll catch you later,' he called back to Tushar.

At the school gate, there was more of the same. This was light-hearted, well-meaning attention. Friends interested to hear about the process and what might be on the horizon for the Khan family. A great fuss was made of Bonzo, and once again everyone called him a wonder dog.

Back at the house, Anwar was just putting his key in the door when a voice from behind him called out, 'Mr Khan? It is Mr Khan, isn't it? This is Bonzo, I believe? I'm with the *Daily Press*. I wonder if I could ask you a few questions.'

'I'm not answering any questions at this time. Would you please leave?' Anwar got into a tangle with his bike, the front door and the dog on his lead. It was all very frustrating and a bit horrible.

Some respite came mid-morning when Sheena O'Shea called.

'Mr Khan – or may I call you Anwar?'

'Anwar, please.'

'Firstly, a big thank-you to you and your family – oh, and of course Bonzo, for coming to our rescue. I have every confidence in the police, but the longer these things go on, the worse it is for everyone. Now, I'm assuming that you've already had a certain amount of interest shown in Bonzo. Maybe even some contact with the press.'

'Yes, I was ambushed on my doorstep this morning.'

'Oh, I am sorry. That is really unfortunate. The very least we can do is help you through this media onslaught. Hopefully we can make things as bearable and maybe as fun as possible.'

'That would be fantastic,' Anwar said with a grateful sigh.

'We've been inundated with requests already. I've got it down to the bare minimum. Hopefully, it won't be too painful.'

'Oh yes?' Anwar replied warily.

'We've divided up all the approaches that have been made into their respective types of media. TV, radio and newspapers including online news. Then there are the various social media platforms which I'll come to in a minute.'

'Crumbs, it all seems to have moved rather rapidly.' Anwar heard the concern in his own voice.

'Don't you worry, that's why I'm here.' Sheena was evidently trying to sound as reassuring as possible. As far as TV goes, we've been approached by *AM: UK*. Have you seen it?'

'We have it on most mornings. In fact, they seem to think Bonzo's already on the schedule.'

'My advice would be to do this one. It's completely non-threatening, everyone is super-friendly and easy-going. You and your wife can accompany Bonzo, and it's just a simple format. You tell the story, they ask a few questions about Bonzo. They all say how lovely he is, give him a pat and you're done.
'Okay, I'll do it, I'm not sure my wife will want to come.'

'Whatever, sweetheart. Now, *AM: UK* has a sister radio station. Normally, whoever does the TV then pops into the radio station and does the same interview. Clearly, a dog guest doesn't make for great radio.'

'No, I can see that, and he's not much of a barker, I'm afraid.'

'That is a good thing, believe me. I'm sure you'll more than make up for him.'

'I'm not sure about that. I've not done anything like this before.'

'You'll be fine, really. As for the newspapers, we'd like to send a photographer round to your house to take a nice family shot. Then the news outlets have got one definitive image that you're happy with, and they can't spin some silly story about you.'

'Spin...?'

'You know, turn it on its head. "Crazy family lets wild dog run loose in public park..."'

'They won't do that, will they?'

'No, I'm kidding. We'll prepare a nice, concise press release to accompany the photo and we're done.'

'Will there be any other TV? The children were asking about *Blue Peter*?'

'Nothing as yet. *Blue Peter* has a bit of a dodgy track record with animals. You only need to type "Blue Peter Elephant" into a YouTube search to see why.'

'Haha, yes, I remember that. Didn't the elephant...'

'Yes, indeed,' she cut him short. 'Social media next and then we're done. I suggest we create an Instagram for Bonzo. *Bonzothedoggy* if it isn't taken, or something like that. People like to feel that they can actually engage. We'll simply have a nice photo of Bonzo and update it from time to time with what he's been doing. We'll also give him a Facebook presence but we'll keep it low key.

'What about Twitter?'

'As you've pointed out, Bonzo hasn't got much to say for himself, so we'll leave Twitter. We don't want him taking on Donald Trump, now, do we?'

'No, I think we've had enough excitement for now.'

Great, I'll get back to the TV station and speak to the photographer. I'll see if we can have the picture taken this evening. I'll also get back to you with details about tomorrow morning. They'll send a car for you, bright and early! We'll speak soon.' Sheena rang off and Anwar called Jen to let her know what was happening.

'You're not taking the kids, it's a school day.'

'I'll ask Andrea to take them to school.'

'What about the dog?'

'He's coming too.'

'Of course, silly me. Okay, I gotta run, big kiss.'

****

Sheena had to discuss a matter with Mr Bradfield. She hurried along to the library, where she found him hard at work in his office, polishing the trophy, now safely back in his custody.

'I'm trying to get the fingerprint powder off. I'm having a tough time. It seems that every time I get a bit off, it then re-sticks itself to another part of the cup.'

'Things could be worse. There could be no cup to clean.'

'Indeed.'

Mr Bradfield... Bernard.' Sheena was at her most charming. 'Tomorrow, our little canine friend is making an appearance on breakfast television.'

'Fantastic, I'll be interested in tuning in and seeing him.'
'Do you remember our conversation with Pete Peters? About how we could turn this whole stressful episode into something positive for the competition next year?

'I do indeed.'

'Tomorrow is our chance to do just that. However, to make the necessary impact, not only do we need the dog, but we also need the cup.'

'No, no way! You're not having it!' Mr Bradfield clutched it to his chest with desperation in his voice.

'Bernard, you have to trust me. We'll take good care of it. We won't let it out of our sight. You can even watch it on television and see for yourself that it's just fine.'

'I didn't sleep for twenty-four – or was it forty-eight hours – oh, I don't know!' He wailed wide-eyed.

'That's all behind us now.'

'But you don't understand. First it was damaged when it was under my care, then I lost it. The strain, the pressure. I tell you, I jolly nearly went mad after that.'

'We've learned a lot from the previous mistak... indiscretions.' She corrected herself. 'This time we'll have everything covered. Security to take it to the studio and bring it back. You've nothing to worry about. What can go wrong? It will be watched by millions.'

'But, but...' Mr Bradfield clung onto the trophy desperately.

'Let me take it off you now.' She let out a little grunt of effort as she prised it out of his grip.' There, you see, I'll put it in its nice case and keep it locked away in my office. It will be back before you know it.'

****

Across London Jago and Finn's plan had gathered pace. They'd pinpointed the *AM: TV* studio. It was situated in a purpose-built glass building, the Gasworks in Gasworks Lane, Shepherds Bush.

'I remember this place when we were little,' Jago said to his brother. They were sitting side by side in Speedy, the green Morris Minor that Muppet had stolen previously. Reluctantly, they'd pressed it into service, not wanting to take any more risks or rent a car. Unknown to them, this gave them an element of invisibility around London because Speedy's old black-and-white number plate could not be read by the city's registration-recognition cameras. Even if Speedy were still listed as stolen and on the police's radar, they'd never spot it.

'It was a wilderness back then. Three high-explosive bombs landed here in the Second World War. When we were boys, it was still a bomb site. The Health and Safety people of today would have had kittens if they'd seen us larking around on it.'

'Now look at it, the la-dee-da Gasworks. All chai lattes and designer beards. Yee-uck,' Finn added.

As they watched, a lorry with 'Location Services' painted on one side backed up to the building. The driver hopped out and pushed an intercom. Slowly a huge shuttered door started to open. The further it opened the more it revealed the inner workings and backstage area of the building.

'There's our way in,' Jago murmured. As they watched, a man with a long khaki coat and a clipboard came out to speak to the driver.

'We just need a couple of those long brown coats, and we'll blend right in,' Finn agreed.

Chapter 9 – Sofa So good

The car arrived on schedule. The last time they'd all been up this early was to catch a budget flight that Jen had booked. That had also been a shock to the system.

The family met in the hallway, Jen and the kids bleary-eyed and pyjamaed. They said their goodbyes and wished the two would-be stars good luck or 'break a leg' as they say in the theatre. Bonzo was looking spruce, having been bathed by the children the night before. His white fur showed up pristine, soft and fluffy against the black. He looked a million dollars, so they made a fuss when he had to go out. Anwar gave him a precautionary walk around the block, and he obliged with a pee and a poop.

'We don't want him making a name for himself on the TV for the wrong reasons,' Anwar joked. With that, he scooped the dog up and kissed Jen and the two children goodbye. The car outside was a people carrier, and the side door slid open automatically when the driver pressed a button.

'Very swish.' Anwar complimented the driver.

'You're in the fast lane now,' the driver quipped back.

They drove northwest across London, making light work of the six miles. It was a joy to drive in London before the rush hour. A rare treat to watch the world go by, passing over Albert Bridge with its view up and down the River Thames, through Chelsea and past Stamford Bridge. Soon they were pulling up in the forecourt of the glass-fronted building.

'Straight into reception there, and they'll sign you in.' The driver pointed to a revolving door. Stationed outside it was a man in a commissionaire's uniform, who saluted Anwar and Bonzo smartly. It was a nice touch.

'Good morning,' a receptionist, whose name badge said she was called Alice, greeted them enthusiastically. 'You're here for...?'

'*AM: TV* with Bill Whitty and Ripley Mitten.'

'Sure, here you are right at the top of the list.' She put a tick by their names. 'I just need a photo of you, sir.'

Anwar posed, there was a click, and a pass for *AM: TV* with Anwar's face on it churned out of a printer. The girl attached it to a lanyard, which he slung around his neck. Then she escorted him and Bonzo to the lift.

'I'll take you to make-up, and then Bill or Ripley will come and say hello in the Green Room.'

'I'm not sure how Bonzo will handle make-up,' Anwar joked.

'He's very well behaved,' Alice observed.
'As long as he can come wherever I'm going, he's usually happy.'

On cue, Bonzo stepped forward and licked the girl's shin.

'He's adorable.' And then to the dog directly, 'And I hear you're such a clever boy,'

The lift gave a ping, and the little party made their way along a corridor. Here Anwar was directed into make-up.

'What's his name?' the make-up girl asked. Anwar told her.

'Shall we give Bonzo a little touch up too? Maybe give him a brush.'

'The poor thing's been brushed to within an inch of his life by my kids. I think we'll hold off.'

The girl finished doing Anwar's make-up and whipped out the tissues she had crammed into the collar of his shirt to keep it clean. He rose from the chair looking as though he had just returned from a holiday in the sun.

In the Green Room, he found that everybody had similar suntans and he grinned sympathetically at the gathering. Bonzo was a big hit with the other guests who had been prepped for their appearances on the morning show.

Anwar was just helping himself to a coffee from a flask when Bill Whitty breezed in.

'Good morning, everyone. I'm Bill.' Everybody knew that. 'I just want to welcome you and let you know a rough running order.'

He introduced himself to a couple seated by the door and asked for the correct pronunciation of their surname. It was a nice touch, and he seemed to lock the information away in his head after repeating it three times.

Anwar was just thinking how dirty Bill's shoes were, wondering if that would show up on the screen. He'd seen him on the TV many times before and never noticed, so probably not.

Bill crossed the room in one gigantic stride and boomed, 'So, this is BON-ZO! What a lovely boy? Girl?'

'Boy,' Anwar confirmed.

'BOY he is,' Bill announced triumphantly. 'Is he friendly?'

'Oh yes, he'll only lick you to death,' Anwar joked.

'Lovely,' Bill intoned. 'What a story, too. Aren't you a clever boy?'

Bonzo, unsurprisingly, did not answer.

'I do have to ask: when we're "live" is he likely to get carried away? You know, jump around, get all barky.'

'I can't guarantee it, but he really is pretty calm. Still, he is a dog.'

Bill smiled and swept out of the room. A large screen bolted to the wall showed him miraculously, and almost instantly, appearing on the sofa next to Ripley.

'I've just been talking to the guests. What a lovely bunch we've got for you this morning.' Bill delivered this line into the kitchens of countless homes around the nation.

One by one the other guests were plucked from the room and eventually it was Anwar and Bonzo's turn. They were snuck into the studio as Tiffany Bloom gave a weather forecast which would turn out later to be embarrassingly wrong. It was often the case.

Bonzo was allowed up on the sofa, and he seemed happy to rest against Anwar. It was an odd feeling to be on this side of the camera. The lights were surprisingly hot and the sofa angular and uncomfortable. It was a scene Anwar knew so well from his kitchen now here he was the other side of the screen. It was strange that there were no people in front of him. Just a bank of robotic cameras and autocue machines against a flat grey wall. Bill was given his cue.

'Our next guest on the sofa some of you may have already heard about. He was certainly all over the papers yesterday. He is something of an unlikely hero. Welcome, Bonzo the Wonder Dog and Anwar his err... person!'

Bill turned to Anwar and enthused, 'You guys have had a busy couple of days.'

'It has been weird, certainly.' Anwar shifted uneasily on the sofa.

'For those of you who don't already know –' Bill looked down the barrel of the camera – 'Bonzo saved next year's Cricket World Cup from potential disaster. Isn't that right, Anwar?'

'I guess so, yes.' Anwar ran his hand through his hair self-consciously.

'Tell us how it happened.'

'We live right near Clapham Common in South London. Every morning we cross it to take our children to school.'

'What are their names?' asked Ripley. 'You'll be in trouble, Dad, if you don't get them a name check!'

'Lita and Zak.' Anwar half-laughed self-consciously. 'After the school drop-off, I normally give Bonzo a bit of a walk. Lately he's been really annoying, rummaging about in the reeds by a pond there. I guess the foxes like to sniff around the ducks there at night. Bonzo went in there the other day and something stung him. We had to take him to the vet, it was really annoying. When I saw him go in there again, I totally freaked out and dived in after him. The next thing I know, we find this metal case.'

'Did you know immediately what it was?' Ripley asked.

'No, not at all. Actually, I tried to get rid of it straight away. Unfortunately, or rather, fortunately, the local bin-men wouldn't take it.'

'That was lucky. And after that, you took it home. Surely that was a bit risky, wasn't it? The police could have accused you of stealing it.'

'I guess so.' Anwar pulled a face. That hadn't occurred to him until now. But everything had moved very quickly, and the organisers had barely made the announcement about the theft before Anwar called them. 'I think they'd have cut me some slack,' he suggested.

'I believe it wasn't until you saw the news that you realised what you had found,' Bill filled in the rest of the story.

'That's right.'

'I believe this is Bonzo's second brush with fame this year?'

They discussed Bonzo's intervention in the Chuck Wagon fire.

'He really has had a busy year,' Ripley said, leaning over to rub Bonzo, who rolled over accommodatingly.

Outside the building, Jago and Finn had been to buy themselves khaki knee-length warehouse coats, then parked in a side road. Now they approached the large shuttered door at the side of the TV building.

'Grab the other end of this,' Jago ordered Finn, motioning to a ladder laid along the side of the forecourt. 'Take it easy, though, remember my leg.' With his injury, he didn't make the most convincing odd-job man.

They picked up the ladder and Jago buzzed the intercom.

'May I help you?' a disembodied voice asked.

'You've locked us out,' Jago said forcefully. 'My mate and me just went to pick up a ladder, we turn around and find you've shut us out.'

There was a click, and the sound of a motor whirring and the shutter began to open.

'Open sesame!' Jago cracked a crooked smile over his shoulder at his brother and led him into the building. It was a cathedral-like space dominated by great blocks of industrial metal venting. Large wheelie-bin dumpsters and wooden crated props lined the walls.

No sooner had the two brothers entered the building than they were accosted by a man who sped up to them on a golf buggy.

'Oi, you two, grab that unit and bring it up to Studio Two,' the harassed looking technician ordered.

Jago and Finn simultaneously put their hands on their chests as if to say, 'Who, me?'

'Yes, you two. Take the service lift and look sharp about it.'

They didn't need telling twice. They pushed and pulled the unit, a hollow block with a logo on one side, into the lift. Jago pressed the button for the second floor and the lift cage shuddered into life.

When the lift door opened by they were greeted by another technician, who was accompanied by a burly man wearing white gloves and holding a large silver trophy.

'Where on earth have you two been? We've been waiting for that.' He pointed to the unit. 'It's for the current news item.'

Jago and Finn carried the block to the edge of the studio. As soon as it was in position the big guy placed the cup on top of it. Jago and Finn were silently shooed away, and the technician gave Bill Whitty a double thumbs up.

Ripley's stroking of Bonzo had been a ploy, a delaying tactic in response to a direction she had received through her earpiece.

'Since we've got the saviour of it here, we thought it would be a good idea to reunite him with the Cricket World Cup.'

Sheena O'Shea, who was watching on her TV at home, rubbed her hands. 'Come on boys, this is the highlight. Sell that World Cup, baby!' she yelled at the set.

'Would you like to come over and join me?' Ripley invited Anwar and Bonzo to follow her over to the side of the studio. Bonzo followed his lead, literally, and hopped off the sofa. He and Anwar took up place next to the trophy, shining on its display unit complete with the 2019 tournament logo.

'I hope you two get to go,' Ripley said as the cameraman framed the shot of the trophy and its unlikely rescuers.

'I'm sure they will. Are you listening, organisers?' Bill joked as he moved on seamlessly to the next item.

'That all went very nicely,' Ripley congratulated the group. 'You were such a good boy.' She bent down and spoke to Bonzo. 'I'd love to take you home.' As she spoke, she ushered them off the set.

Jago and Finn had been leaning against a wall watching the proceedings. It was fascinating to see the goings-on behind the scenes on television. The big guy with the gloves retrieved the World Cup and brushed past them. Jago gave Finn a nudge and then nodded at the trophy.

Alice appeared and spoke to Anwar. 'I'm going to take you over to the radio studio now.'

'Is there any chance I could pop into the washroom before we go?' he asked sheepishly.

'Sure, it's just there. I'll come back for you in a minute.'

'Could you just hold my dog for a moment?' Anwar asked the guy in the white gloves, holding out Bonzo's lead.

'Err... Okay, I guess so,' he grumbled, setting the trophy down gently on the ground. He turned back and took the leash.

'Thanks a lot. I'll just be a second.'

The big man looked faintly ridiculous with the little dog attached to one hand.

Jago hobbled over to him.

'Look, big fella, you've enough on your hands. I'll look after the dog.'

'That's very kind of you,' said the man in the white gloves, turning to Jago. As he did so, Finn deftly removed the trophy. Jago did a good job of making a mess of the Bonzo handover. By the time the minder had extracted himself from the tangle of the dog's lead Finn had disappeared down the corridor.

'What the...?' he exclaimed, half-starting to run down the corridor.

At that moment the lift opened, and Jago swept up Bonzo and stepped into it. A corridor that moments ago had been a hive of activity was suddenly empty, except for the hapless keeper of the World Cup.

Jago watched the lights of the lift as they ticked through the floors. The doors opened, and once again he found himself in the bowels of the building. As he stepped out of the lift, Finn burst through a pair of double swing doors. He'd apparently been running hard. He slid side-saddle down the banister of the stairs leading to the loading bay.

'To the golf buggy!' Jago declared as Finn made his landing perfectly like a gymnast. Finn stowed the trophy on the back, and Jago eased himself into the passenger seat holding Bonzo close to his chest. The dog made no protest; it wasn't in his nature. As Finn hopped in and gunned the accelerator, to Bonzo it was just another adventure that might end up in a walk. A large red button marked 'SHUTTER' let them out and they careered off into the distance to their getaway car.

Inside the building, the fallout from the brothers' actions was just starting to take its effect. When Anwar re-emerged from the washroom, he was surprised to find the corridor empty. Alice re-appeared.

'Shall we go?' she asked brightly.

'We could, but my dog seems to have disappeared.'

The big guy came lumbering back down the corridor. 'Did you see the removal man in the brown coat?' he asked.

'What removal man?' Anwar and Alice said in unison.

The building's security cameras had recorded the whole sorry tale. The station that put out the news was about to become the news.

Chapter 10 – Handsome Ransom

DC Palmer had convened a meeting of all the aggrieved parties. Now they were assembled in a conference room at the television studio.

Mr Bradfield had received the news that the trophy had been stolen, again, as calmly as possible. It wasn't until he put the telephone down that he experienced something close to heart failure. Despite this shock to his system he had managed to get himself into a taxi to make the relatively short journey.

The video files had been loaded onto a laptop, and everyone crowded around behind the policeman to view them.

'We've got the footage from the loading bay, the corridor and the perimeter gate.'

Anwar, Mr Bradfield and the TV station's head of security, Reg Stryker, leaned over as the first clip was played.

'You can see them making their entry through the main loading bay. They don't seem to be challenged in any way,' DC Palmer explained.

Mr Stryker shifted uneasily behind him as they watched the stuttering footage.

'The first interaction they have is with this individual on the golf cart.'

The little vehicle appeared to whizz over to the pair.

'It's amazing that he just lets them in,' commented DC Palmer.

'We do have a high volume of casual staff. People who are working on short-term contracts. Their references are all carefully checked,' Stryker retorted defensively.

'We're not looking to blame anyone. At this stage we just want to confirm the identity of the offenders.'

'Do you have an idea who they are?' Anwar said hopefully.

'All in the fullness of time, sir. Let's watch the rest of the footage.'

DC Palmer clicked the next file on the laptop.

'We have them passing down the corridor from the lift on the second floor. The suspects are carrying some sort of box. At first I thought this was how they got the trophy out.'

'No,' Anwar broke in. 'They brought it onto the studio floor, I saw them.'

'Yes, it seems they were hiding in plain sight.'

'What does that mean?' asked Mr Bradfield.

'They made themselves unnoticeable by staying visible,' DC Palmer explained. 'The next time we have them on the move, they execute what appears to be a well-practised manoeuvre. We've watched it several times, even in slow motion. It's rather beautiful.'

'You can't be serious?' Bradfield broke in, irritation in his voice.

'Sorry, Mr Bradfield. But, in the course of a day, I see many senseless crimes. Finding one with a bit of invention is refreshing. Watch this. The first suspect appears to take the dog, there is a mix-up with the lead and... There we go, in comes suspect number two, and he's away with the trophy. Off goes the security guard in pursuit, but he's got a start on him. Meanwhile, number one steps into the lift and he's away. What he doesn't realise is... Smile for the camera.' Palmer paused the footage. 'There, we have a beautifully framed picture of him stepping into the lift. Hello, Jago.'

'Do you know this man, officer?' Mr Bradfield asked.

'I do indeed. It's Jago, and if I'm not mistaken, his brother, Finn O'Toole. We had already identified them as suspects in the jewellery shop robbery. I'd just been waiting for a positive match on fingerprints taken from tools found at the scene of the crime. A perfect match for the two of them.'

'Does that mean you have an address for them?' Anwar asked hopefully.

'It does, but I think it's fair to say they'll be lying low somewhere else for a bit. If we watch the last bit of footage...' DC Palmer tapped the laptop again. 'Here they are making their way down Gasworks Lane on the golf cart. Then a couple of minutes later we have the getaway car.' Again he paused the film framing the Morris Minor and its distinctive registration.

'How do you know it's them? It could be anyone,' Mr Bradfield reasoned.

'Because Gasworks Lane is a dead end.'

'Does that mean you'll catch them?'

'It means we stand a very good chance,' DC Palmer replied cagily.

****

Some distance from West London, that outcome was looking increasingly likely. While it had seemed a good idea to acquire a wonder dog, the O'Tooles hadn't counted on him working against them. They'd made their way out of London past Heathrow Airport. Just off the motorway, they'd tried to get a room in several chain hotels. All of them had denied the fugitives a room on account of their no-pet policy. Getting increasingly desperate, they had finally managed to access the Internet in a coffee shop. Through it, they had found a room in a B&B owned by a Mr and Mrs Mildwater, on the outskirts of Windsor.

'Of course, you can bring your dog, lovey,' Mrs Mildwater had said when telephoned. 'I've got three. The more, the merrier.'
When they got there, they found that the B&B was a rambling house that had seen better days. The Mildwaters were both in their seventies and let rooms to supplement their pension.

Much to the brothers' relief, there was a tumbledown garage where they were able to park the car. They left the trophy stowed in the car's boot.

'Bring your bags in through the kitchen,' called the old lady, who was leaning on the bottom half of the kitchen's stable door. 'I've put you in the pink room.'

'Very nice, I'm sure,' Jago replied gruffly, not wanting to be drawn into a conversation.

'Oh, but you've hurt your foot. Will you be able to manage the stairs?'

'I'll be just fine.'

Finn joined him, having got the dog off the back seat.

'Here he is,' the old woman gushed. 'What's his name?'

'B...' Finn started.

'...Ernie,' Jago finished.

'Bernie,' they said together.

'Would he like to meet my three? DOGGIES!' the old lady cried. There was a scrabbling of paws and the closed bottom of the back door was buffeted vigorously. There was also a good deal of aggressive barking.

Bonzo crouched down and would not budge. He was an extremely sociable hound. Normally this action was to ensure that he didn't miss the opportunity to say hello to any potential new friends. Here it was taken as him being frightened.

'I'm not sure he likes the sound of your dogs,' said Finn. 'He's just a little fella, after all.'

'Oh dear, perhaps you're right. Would you like to take him round to the front door?'

'Come along, Bernie,' Finn coaxed him, dragging Bonzo by his lead. The little dog had spread himself into a star shape and was being bodily pulled along.

'He's very determined, isn't he?' Mrs Mildwater observed.

'Pick it up,' Jago hissed to his brother.

At the front door, the brothers rang an old bell with a rope attached to the clapper. Its ring brought Mr Mildwater to the door.

'No, thank you, I never buy anything on the doorstep. Goodbye,' he said vaguely.
'We're your lodgers,' Finn ventured. 'The ones with the dog, remember?'

'Cecil, let them in,' his wife scolded him fiercely, appearing at the back of the hall. Both the brothers recoiled slightly. 'He's such a silly old fool,' she added, turning the charm back on. 'Your room is at the top of the stairs on the right. Would you like supper?'

'That would be grand,' said Finn, who couldn't remember when they'd last had a decent meal. Letting Bonzo lead them, the two men disappeared upstairs.

'Phew, what a nightmare!' Jago gasped as he threw himself down on one of the single beds in the room. 'They didn't mention the free annoying chit-chat that comes with the room.'

'We'll all be old someday.' Finn took a more sympathetic view.

'Don't you go getting soft on me, not now. We're in this thing pretty deep.'

'What about the dog?' Finn asked.

'What d'ya mean what about the dog? It's a flaming wonder dog. We get money for it! Money for the dog, and money for the trophy. We've got a double whammy here. Did you hear what they were saying about that cricket competition on the telly? It would be a disaster not to have the trophy. Well, unless I'm much mistaken, they haven't got the trophy, have they? They'll pay anything to get it back.'

'I meant what about the dog's dinner,'
'For goodness' sake!' Jago burst out. 'Very well, go out and buy the dog some food. While you're about it, get a newspaper, some kids' glue and a notepad.'

Finn did as he was told. Mr Mildwater explained that there was a general store with a post office inside it at the end of the street. Finn followed his directions and had no problems finding the shop and picking up everything they needed from its odd assortment of stock. In no time he was back at Mildwater Towers.

'I've got everything,' he said as he closed the door of the pink room behind him.

'Good. We need to send a ransom note. We'll make it out of the newspaper like they do in the films. You know, cut letters out and make words with them.'

'Won't that take an awfully long time?' asked Finn.

'We've nothing better to do, now, have we?'

By now Bonzo was out of sorts. There had been no walk. He didn't like the humans he was with. He missed his own people. Why had they left him? It was all so hard to understand. He squirmed his way under a writing table, and there he stayed.

Back in Clapham the news of his disappearance had not been well received. The tears had stopped, but Lita was still clinging to Jen, red-faced, her body heaving with intermittent sobs.

'What kind of low-life steals a family dog?' Anwar shook his head disbelievingly.

'We'll get him back, though, Dad, won't we?' Zak asked.

'Of course, son. We just need to be patient that's all.' Deep down, though, Anwar couldn't be sure. They were obviously dealing with some pretty brazen and dodgy characters. Who knew what they were capable of doing? It was best not to dwell on it.

'Tell you what, let's order pizza and watch a film.'

Grudgingly, everyone agreed.

Back along the M4 motorway, dinner with the Mildwaters was a little more formal. The O'Toole brothers were summoned to the table by the ringing of a small gong. When they arrived for dinner, Mr Mildwater was already installed in the formal dining room.

'Each of you, take a place,' Mrs Mildwater fussed. The two brothers took their seats. They were each given a plate with a blue Chinese pattern and a crack that appeared to have been glued.

'Help yourself, dear,' she said to Finn as if he were thirteen. He reached forward and took a sausage and a dollop of potato.

The sausages were only part cooked, pink and raw in the middle, while the mashed potato had blackish lumps in it. Stewed cabbage was something neither of them had eaten since they were children.

Mr Mildwater had a big yellow book propped up beside him. He smoothed a hand over the slab of grey hair plastered to his head and turned a page of *Wisden Cricketers' Almanack*. Mrs Mildwater did not join them. Consequently, the brothers struggled to eat the food in silence, kicking each other under the table to make the other laugh.

The plates were cleared and the pudding arrived, a trifle in a glass bowl. It was no less horrific than the first course. Jago found a piece of cotton in his serving. Finn, meanwhile, found the needle.

'May we help with the washing up?' Finn offered as Mrs Mildwater cleared their dessert plates.

'Don't be silly,' she scolded.

'In that case, I think we'll take the little dog for a walk around the block.'

'I just let my dogs out into the garden. You're sure you don't want to try...?'

'I think it's best we keep him in one piece, don't you?'

The Mildwaters gave them a poop bag and a key to the front door, and the two men left the house with Bonzo. Following a street map on Jago's phone, they made their way away from the house.

'Are you going to be all right with that foot of yours?' asked Finn.

'Anything to get out of that madhouse.' Jago snorted, consulting his phone. 'We go straight along here and then take the second right,' he directed. The sun was setting and as they walked the glow from the phone's screen showed on his face.

'Are we going to see the castle, maybe see if Her Madge is in?'

'No, we aren't making any detours.'

They walked on until they got to Windsor Police Station. Jago took a folded piece of paper out of his pocket and passed it to Finn.

'Take it in, will you?'

'I will not! You take it in.'

'I've got this.' Jago pointed to his booted foot.

'Go on, then, give it to me,' Finn said grudgingly. With that, he nipped into the police station. There was an unattended window and a buzzer. Finn left the piece of paper on the counter, pushed the button and then legged it.

'Let's go,' Finn urged Jago as soon as he reached him. They walked away as fast as the booted foot would allow. Soon they were on a quiet residential street.

'There doesn't seem to be anything special about this so-called wonder dog,' Finn said conversationally. He looked at Bonzo who had stretched the lead to its fullest extent so that he could sniff a lamp post.

'Try him out. Give him an order,' Jago suggested.

'Okay. Bonzo, sit,' Finn started.

'SIT? Any pooch will sit,' Jago scoffed. But Bonzo hadn't sat.

'Sit!' Finn tried again. Bonzo resolutely ignored him.

'Useless pooch,' Jago sneered.

With that, Bonzo sat firmly on the ground.

'There's a good boy,' Finn said, bending down. Bonzo winked at him. 'Did you see that?' Finn exclaimed. 'He winked at me.'

'He did not.'

'I tell you, he did,' Finn let go of the lead and put both hands on his hips, a double teapot as cricket commentators call it, to show his frustration.

Bonzo took full advantage of being released and bolted.

'Get after him, you idiot!' Jago ranted.

Finn did as he was told and sprinted down the road. Smart or not, Bonzo had managed to outwit the O'Toole brothers. They wandered the streets for the next hour without success. Eventually, they gave up and returned to the B&B. They walked to the back of the house. At the back door, they were surprised to find Mrs Mildwater sitting on the back step. Bonzo was at her feet, her hand resting on his head.

'It seems he doesn't like you two that much,' Mrs Mildwater observed.

'He likes us just fine,' Jago said gruffly. 'Now if you'll excuse us, I think it's time we said good night.' He took Bonzo's lead and dragged him past the old lady.

'Have a peaceful night and a perfect end,' she called after them, quoting a night prayer.

'What did she mean by *a perfect end*?' Finn said as they climbed the stairs.

'It means she thinks you have a nice bum.'

Really?'

'Of course not. How should I know what she means? The woman's as mad as a snake.' With that, the brothers settled down for the night with Bonzo, in the pink room.

Across town, despite the late hour, the Windsor Police had communicated the contents of the brothers' message to the wider police network.

Chapter 11 – Bad News Travels Fast

DC Palmer had put a call in to the Khans as soon as he received the news. It had been late but he was sure they'd want to hear that there was some news of Bonzo. That was something positive at least and might help them sleep.

His call to Mr Bradfield the following morning did nothing to reassure him as to how things were working out.

'I knew it! The blighters. What do we do now?'

'We tread very carefully. It is doubtful that these men will get away with this. Both of them have records and have spent time at Her Majesty's pleasure.' This was a polite way of saying they were criminals who knew the consequences of what they did. Both had been to prison, and no doubt would be heading there again. 'The dog complicates matters. He is a hostage and we want to make sure he is returned to his family unscathed. If we corner them and they get desperate... Well, let's just say I'd like to avoid that situation.'

'Absolutely, I quite understand. What should I do now?'

'We do have something to go on. The note was handed in to Windsor Police. We therefore know that they either passed through Windsor or are holed up in the area. In a case like this, the public can be our eyes and ears. The newspapers will have their say, but not until tomorrow. The rolling news on TV, radio and the Internet will run it. The Twitter-sphere will pick it up too. For the public to be engaged, we need to get information out there. We need good images and descriptions of the suspects. That goes for the dog, too. He's a compact little guy, and they could carry him about in a bag if necessary. We have to hope that they make a mistake and someone spots them.'

'From Windsor, they could have carried on down the motorway to Bristol, Cornwall, Wales, anywhere. Oh dear, it really is rather daunting.'

'The chances are they won't go too far. They've lived in South London their whole lives. I can't see them running off to Timbuktu. They won't go home either. The heat is on, and they won't go back until things have cooled off. We've got our people watching their house too, so if they are that daft...'

'As far as the ransom note goes, I suppose that was aimed at us,' Mr Bradfield speculated.

The Khans love their dog but I doubt they can stretch to half a million.'

'Yes, indeed. That figure sounds intended for a large organisation. I'll need to speak to Mr Peters and Miss O'Shea to discuss what action we are going to take. We'll need your advice too, DC Palmer. Obviously they won't be forced into paying a ransom but we need a considered response.'

The two men agreed to speak later and ended their call.

****

Anwar, back in Clapham, had been able to wake the children with the good news about Bonzo.

'Will he be home today, Daddy?' asked Zak.

'No, not today. Soon, hopefully.'

'I don't want to go to school, then,' Lita said firmly.

'If Lita's not going to school, then I'm not going either,' Zak joined in.

'Hold on a minute, nobody is missing school.' Anwar laid down the law. 'In any case, Lita, you have your school trip today.

You've been looking forward to it. What's more, I've made you a magnificent packed lunch and I do not want to waste it.'

The children dragged their feet, but eventually they all made it out of the house.

'Leaving Bonzo at home today, kids?' boomed Loud Dunc on his way past.

Lita instantly burst into tears.

'Sorry, mate, did I say something wrong?' Loud Dunc spoke a little more quietly and looked concerned.

'Don't worry. I'll explain later,' a strained-looking Anwar replied.

Despite this hiccup, Anwar eventually steered the children across the common. Zak stowed his bike and made his way into the school. Lita joined the queue leading up to a parked coach.

'Mrs Thompson, would you keep an eye on Lita? She's had a bit of bad news and has been a bit teary,' he confided in one of the teachers.

'Of course. She'll be fine once we get going. They're all very excited.'

Anwar left Lita framed in one of the windows of the coach. She refused to react to his pulled faces. As the coach drew away, he swung a leg over his bike and pedalled home.

****

Faces were being pulled in Pete Peters' office too. Inside the corporate glass cube, the air conditioning blew a chill wind that matched the executive's mood. Through the window, groundsmen could be seen hard at work putting the cricket ground's pitches to bed for the winter. Bathed in warm September sun their job looked a lot more appealing. The overnight news meant that the competition's organisers were wrestling with a grim ultimatum.

'What do the police advise, Bradfield?'

'DC Palmer says there are three main things to think about. The biggest one is trust. Both sides are going to be suspicious of the other. The next is bargaining, and the final one is how the agreed transaction is carried out.'

'We're not actually going to pay these guys?' Sheena exclaimed.

'I think the idea is to come to a mutually agreeable arrangement,' Mr Bradfield said calmly.

'But to do all these things we need to make contact, with the bad guys on the one hand and the public on the other,' Sheena pointed out.

'Precisely, and this is where you come in, Sheena. We want to make the most of this publicity. If we build the competition, they will come,' he said grandly as if he was making a historic speech. 'Add to that our people's hero, Bonzo, to help focus the story. Of course, that depends on getting him back safely.'

All the time he was speaking, Sheena was writing feverishly. Her pen crossed the paper in great sweeps. She paused for a moment.

'At this rate, people may start to think we keep losing the trophy on purpose.'

'You're not, are you?' Mr Bradfield asked, looking a little shocked.

'Of course not,' Pete scolded him.

'Okay, I've got this,' Sheena broke in, turning her pad round for the two men to see.

'World Cup and Hero snatched. Cricket World Cup countdown. London Police launch manhunt,' she read aloud as their eyes followed the lines.

'Covers all the main points. Short and direct,' Pete observed.

'Wise not to mention it's the second time. That would make us look a tiny bit careless,' Bradfield commented.

A press release was duly drawn up. It made an appeal for the public to be the eyes and ears of the police. To watch for any unusual activity, any leads that might help to solve the crime. There was a nice picture of Bonzo and another of the trophy, along with a helpline contact number for people to get in touch with any information.

The press release was circulated through the various news outlets. The stirring language struck the right note, and the reaction to it was quick and encouraging.

Soon Sheena was posting an emailed update to her colleagues.

'Great traction with the press. Already we are trending on Twitter, and we've had two sightings of the dog. One in Giggleswick and another in Aberystwyth. Clearly, we will have our fair share of false alarms but the police are happy with the response so far.'

'Good job, Sheen. Keep me updated,' Pete Peters' response was brief and to the point.

****

Technology was not a concern at the Mildwaters'. The O'Toole brothers couldn't complain about the speed of the Wi-Fi because there was no Wi-Fi. It was frustrating and perfect at the same time. By chance, they had found the most anonymous hideout possible. There were a few frustrations, of course. The old people tended to have the television on in the kitchen constantly, with the volume set to max. Wherever you were in the house, you could hear the TV droning in the background. Add to that the incredible amount of dog fluff everywhere. Wherever the brothers sat down, they were covered in the stuff.

As for their hosts, Mr Mildwater seemed indifferent to them. He bumbled around and would shut himself away to read. Mrs Mildwater, however, despite her advancing years was... Well, it was difficult to put your finger on just what it was about Mrs Mildwater. *Feisty* was the word the brothers came up with in the end. The tiny little woman bustled about, her hair scraped back in a grey bun. Both the men did their best to keep out of her way. She was either quick to scold or over-chatty.

They'd stayed in their room to avoid having their ears bent with another rambling, repetitive story.

'Come on, we need to get out.' Jago gave Finn a nudge.

'Where to?'

'We have an errand. Anyway, your mutt needs a walk as well.'

Finn picked Bonzo up and they crept out of their room. They edged down the stairs knowing the slightest creak would bring Mrs Mildwater down on them. The bottom step gave them away and she came bustling out.

'A bit of a slow start to the day for you gentleman. Poor Bernie will be desperate, the little love.'

'We're just going out now, so if you'll excuse us.' Jago made a lunge for the front door.

'Just you make sure you give him a good walk. He may have little legs but...'

The brothers closed the door on her and missed the last instruction.

'How many times did she tell us off in two minutes? It's worse than our ma,' Finn said, puffing his cheeks out.

'Get your cap on and your sunglasses,' Jago ordered. 'Remember, we're supposed to be incognito.'

'Where are we going?'

'We need to get a prepaid SIM card at the supermarket. It's time we got in touch to discuss terms. Give us the money or the little guy gets it, mmmwwwahahaha!' Jago put on a jokey maniacal laugh and drew his finger across his throat.

'Easy, Jago,' Finn hugged Bonzo to him. 'You're not serious, are you?'

'Maybe I am, and maybe I'm not. I'm on the edge, Finn. They shouldn't mess with me.'

'Are we going to Tesco or Sainsbury's?' Finn changed the subject.

They were on their way to a playing field where they'd walked the dog before.

'Look, they've got prepaid SIM cards in there.' Finn pointed to a corner shop.

There was a very unofficial-looking sign written in black felt pen and stuck in the window.

'It'll save us dragging all the way over to the big store. Fewer people, too. Well spotted.'

There was a similar sign that stated 'no dogs', so Finn waited outside with Bonzo.

Inside, the shopkeeper rummaged about under the counter for the advertised cards. Over his shoulder, there was a TV playing a rolling news channel. Jago watched it blankly until the news ticker bar at the bottom of the screen caught his eye.

'Police release helpline number for news relating to missing Cricket World Cup.'

Jago took out his phone and typed the number into it.

'They'll nick anything, some people.' The shopkeeper nodded at the screen.

'Yeah, terrible, isn't it?' Jago looked shifty for a moment. 'You wouldn't mind giving me a hand with this?'

The distraction worked, and the shopkeeper helped him fit the new card.

Back outside the shop, Jago told Finn the news.

'I think it's time to get in touch, don't you?'

They walked the short distance to the playing field. Finn let Bonzo off the lead and the dog was happy to sprint around in search of exciting smells. The two brothers sat on a nearby pair of swings. Jago wrapped his arms around the swing's chains and tapped out the number he'd seen on the shop's television. The brothers swung idly while the connection was made.

'Police helpline. How may I direct your call?'

'We have a situation. I guess I need to speak to the officer in charge.'

'May I ask what this is about?'

'I have the trophy and the dog. I'm calling to discuss our demands.'

'May I take a name?'

'A name...?' the question took Jago aback for a moment. A discarded ice-cream wrapper on the ground prompted him. 'Magnum,' he said mysteriously.

'Thank you, Mr Magnum. Please hold.'

'What the...?' Jago looked at the handset in disbelief that they were messing him around.

In reality, the chance of him being put straight through to the officer in charge of the case was a remote one. The call worked its way through the police system like a pinball on a table. The line whirred and clicked with static. Eventually, the telephone on DC Palmer's desk gave a long shrill ring.

'DC Palmer speaking,'

'Youse took your time,' Jago barked.

'I'm speaking to Mr Magnum, I believe?'

'Cut the mister, it's Magnum, just MAG-NUM.'

'Okay, noted. How may I help you, Magnum?'

'It's time to make the handover,' Jago informed him.

'Is that right?'

'Yep. I'll tell you when and where.'

'Now, hold on, you see it doesn't quite work like that...' began DC Palmer, but Jago ended the call.

'Cheeky monkey,' Jago fumed to no one in particular and redialled the number. This time he was put straight through to the DC without having to introduce himself.

'Do I have your attention now?' he demanded. 'There'll be no "hold on", do I make myself clear?'

'Absolutely, my apologies. I was just trying to establish a couple of facts. We've had a number of false alarms. As you may imagine, a case like this attracts national interest.'
'Now we've established that I am who I say I am,' Jago continued.

'If you don't mind, is there any way that you could prove that you have the dog and that he's –' DC Palmer swallowed – 'alive?'

'For goodness sake,' Jago muttered to himself. 'Oi,' he hissed to Finn, holding the handset away from his mouth. 'Go and get the dog and bring him over here, will ya?'

Finn did as he was told. Bonzo took a little bit of rounding up, but before long Finn had caught the dog and carried him over to his brother.

'I'm going to put him on the line now,' Jago said to DC Palmer. 'Speak,' he urged Bonzo.

'We've not heard him utter so much as a woof yet,' Finn reasoned.

'Come on, speak, will ya?' Jago tried again.

Bonzo gave the handset a good lick.

'Hello,' a tiny voice called out from the phone. Jago put it to his ear, grimacing at the Bonzo spit with which it was covered.

'I'm guessing that was the dog, not you,' DC Palmer continued.

'Yes, it was the hostage,' Jago replied trying to get back into character as Magnum.

'Thank you for that; obviously a transaction of this kind relies on trust.'

'I'm trusting you've got your side of the bargain in order.'

'We've looked at your demands,' DC Palmer explained. 'But I'm afraid we still haven't been able to get all the relevant parties to sign off on it.'

'Nonsense, you're stalling. I'm not some two-bit chancer, I'm the real deal, yer hear?' As Jago spoke, Finn caught his attention drawing an imaginary rectangle in the air and tapping his wrist.

'What is it?' Jago put his hand over the mobile phone.

'The old folks' TV in the kitchen. If we don't get back, they'll see the lunchtime time news and they're bound to call the cops.'

Jago gave him a thumbs up.

'I have to go,' he told DC Palmer. 'You just do what you have to do to sort it. I'll be in touch, tomorrow, at ten o'clock.'

'No, wait,' DC Palmer called down the line but he was too late. 'Can we call the number back? He asked an assistant who'd been listening in.
They tried, but Jago had already slipped the SIM card out of the phone.

'Useless!' DC Palmer snapped.

Back in Windsor, the brothers had jogged as best they could back to the Mildwaters' house. Bonzo had enjoyed the run, happy to keep up with the pace. They burst through the front door, much to the surprise of Mrs Mildwater. She was dusting cobwebs from the ceiling in the hallway with a long feather duster.

'My goodness, you nearly gave me a heart attack,' she cried.

'Sorry about that, Mrs M,' Finn apologised.

'Call of nature,' blurted Jago and pushed past them both. He made his way into the kitchen. There he found the small television talking away to itself. Mrs Mildwater had now moved on to hoovering, so he was able to turn the set off without it being noticed. He pulled open some drawers and on the third attempt found the cutlery and a pair of scissors. He unplugged the TV, cut its cable, then put the plug back into the socket.

'Would you like a cup of tea?' he shouted over the din of the hoover to Mrs Mildwater, who was returning to the hallway.

'Yes, dear, that would be lovely. I'll drink it while I watch the news.'

But there would be no news. The world's most over-used telly wasn't working any more.

'I wonder what's got into it?' Mrs Mildwater complained, pushing all the buttons on the remote. 'It was fine this morning.'

'They can be very temperamental things, foreign tellies,' Jago sympathised.

'Cecil,' Mrs Mildwater called out.

'Yes, dear?' Mr Mildwater enquired as he put his head around the door.

'The television has gone wrong. We need to get the man in.'

'Yes, dear,' he replied and disappeared from view.

Life in the Mildwater house was much more peaceful without the constant drone of the television. Nobody seemed to miss it. It was more background noise than anything. Company for Mrs Mildwater, perhaps.

After the excitement of the morning, time passed slowly in the brothers' self-imposed prison. By mid-afternoon, Finn had had enough.

'I'm going stir-crazy here, Jago,' he said to his brother, who was reading the paper with his feet up.

'Calm down. Some people would pay a fortune for a rest like this,' Jago replied.

'The dog looks fed up too. I'm going to take him back out.'

'Keep your head down then and wear your hat.'

'I will, but it's not as if anybody knows we're here.'

****

Across town, however, Old Town Junior School's trip to Windsor Castle had just come to an end. The children had just left the learning centre outside the castle walls and were getting onto their coach.

'What's in the bag, Lita?' Mr Honey, one of the accompanying teachers, asked.

'A Windsor Castle notepad and a keyring. They were both reduced,' Lita said proudly.

'Who'd have thought the Queen would have a sale?' her teacher joked.

Lita suspected the Queen didn't make decisions like that, but she liked Mr Honey so she smiled pleasantly. She made her way along the aisle to a window seat halfway down the coach. A crowd bottleneck was building up at the door as some of the children fussed about where they wanted to sit.

'Come along, children, the driver needs to get going.' Mr Honey chivvied everyone along. 'Just sit down wherever you are.'

Rosie Cheek, who wasn't a particular friend of Lita's, plonked herself next to her.

'What was your best bit?' Rosie asked her randomly.

'The Queen's doll's house, I think,' Lita replied.

'I wanted to see Meghan Markle,' said Rosie dreamily, and with that their conversation came to an end.

Lita was happy to watch the world go by through the window. It had been a long day, and her eyelids were starting to get heavy. The coach had pulled away from the car park and was now heading out of the town. At a zebra crossing, it came to a halt for a pedestrian with a great hiss of brakes and the noise jolted Lita out of her daze. She looked out of the window and saw a man in a baseball cap walking towards her along the pavement. At first she didn't notice that he had a dog on a lead – and then Bonzo stepped out from behind him.

Lita's eyes widened, her mouth dropped open and then her voice came.

'BON-ZO!' She banged on the window with both fists for all she was worth.

Mr Honey was out of his seat and down the aisle in an instant. By now the coach had lurched off, and Bonzo and his handler were receding into the distance.

'What on earth is all the fuss about, Lita?' asked Mr Honey, concern etched on his face.

'MY DOGG-Y!' she bawled.

'Don't worry, I'll take over,' said Mrs Thompson, appearing at his shoulder. 'Now, what is it, Lita?'

'Look, it's Bonzo, my Bonzo.' She jabbed the glass with her finger.

Mrs Thompson looked through the window but by now they were well on their way.

'Rosie, would you mind if I sit here? Mr Honey will find you a seat.' Mrs Thompson sat in the seat next to Lita and tried to calm her down but she would have none of it.

By the time they were back at school, they were both worn out, one from fretting and the other from coping with it. Anwar was waiting outside the school with some of the other parents when the coach pulled up.

'Mr Khan, I'm afraid Lita's had a bit of a shock.' Mrs Thompson explained.

'Daddy!' She yanked at his sleeve. 'I saw him, I saw Bonzo. You have to believe me.'

Anwar called Jen and she came home from work early. Normally, the sound of her key in the door would stir Bonzo into action. There would be the scrabbling sound of his claws on the kitchen floor as he tried to launch himself to greet her. Today, there was just the click of the latch. The house seemed oddly quiet without him. Jen found Anwar and Lita in the kitchen. Lita was lying curled up in Bonzo's bed. Jen addressed her as if it were the most normal thing in the world.

'You're sure it was him?'

'Cross my heart,' Lita replied, stroking one of Bonzo's toys, Brenda the beaver, that lay in her lap.

Jen shared a look with Anwar, who was standing with his back against the sink. They needed no words to communicate.

He pushed himself away from the sink and left the room. Jen bent down and stroked Lita's hair.

'Shall we go and find Zak? Come on, give me your hand.'

Lita reached a hand up and allowed herself to be pulled to her feet.

In the living room, Anwar called a mobile number that DC Palmer had given him.

'Hi, it's err... Anwar Khan here. Bonzo's dad.'

'Yes, Anwar. Dave Palmer speaking.'

'I know it sounds totally off the wall, but we've seen Bonzo. Not we as such, my daughter. He was on the street in Windsor.'

Anwar realised that Lita's word sounded less believable than an adult's. But he hadn't taken into consideration the fact that DC Palmer was a dad too. He didn't automatically dismiss it as the imagination of a child. It was too elaborate a story to be purely make-believe.

'Windsor, you say? That is indeed a chance in a million. It ties in with the information that we have on the suspects to date. I'll let my colleagues in the area know. Let's speak again tomorrow.'

Later that evening Anwar and Jen had flopped onto the sofa. It was a relief to veg out and watch some mindless TV. They flicked through the channels and eventually settled on an old movie. It was to prove oddly serendipitous.

Chapter 12 – Sting in the Tail

Colleagues often joked behind his back that Bernard Bradfield's first name was actually 'Mister'. It wasn't that he had a superiority complex, he was just rather particular about things and a tiny bit uptight. In the office washroom, he looked at his reflection in the mirror. This morning's meeting with Pete Peters was important. He should look his best and he straightened his Primary Club tie. The Primary Club is a charity for the visually impaired, open to anyone who has been out first ball in any form of cricket. He hoped that later he wouldn't be bowled a metaphoric 'googly' and be given 'out' by Pete. He pushed his way through the door marked "OUT". It corresponded to the "IN" on the entrance door. It was a joke for the cricket lover, that always made him smile, but today it made him shudder.

Pete Peters spotted him through the glass door of the World Cup office and waved him into the cube. Sheena was already there, her chin rested on her folded hands. It was a pose that gave nothing away.

'Ah, Bernard.' Pete welcomed him.

Calling me Bernard? That's not a good sign, he thought to himself. 'Bernard' suggested the impending delivery of cataclysmic news. It was a 'hey Bernard, we're all in this together' opening.

'You've heard, I take it, that those dastardly villains have got in contact.'

'That is why we're here, no?'

'Indeed.'

Sheena piped up. 'What Pete is trying to say, Bernard, is that the competition organisers – our bosses, that power far greater than any of us – have also been in touch.'

'Oh yes.' Mr Bradfield shifted nervously. He couldn't help but feel that this run of bad fortune traced a direct route back to him.

'I'll cut to the heart of the matter. It seems that they aren't too keen on stumping up the cash,' Sheena explained.

'What?'

'They're in no mood to bargain. They feel that if they pay up, then everyone will start doing it.' Pete explained their excuse.

'They can't just say no, surely?'

'That seems to be just what they're saying.' Sheena shrugged.

'We'll know more when DC Palmer arrives. He will advise us, and as you know we're expecting another call from this Magnum, as he calls himself, at ten o'clock.' Pete checked his watch.

Mr Bradfield turned away and rubbed his temples. The groundsmen were having a tea break in one of the lawn-mower sheds across the practice ground. He wished his life were as straightforward. Behind him, the glass door opened and DC Palmer accompanied by Anwar joined the group.

'A penny for your thoughts.' DC Palmer touched him lightly on the arm. It brought him back to the present moment. 'Have you met Anwar Khan, Bonzo the dog's owner?' He introduced Anwar, who had accompanied him.

'Take a seat, gentlemen.' Sheena invited them to sit at a table in the middle of which was a telephone for conference calls. Through this several people could listen to a call at the same time.

'One moment, Sheena.' Pete Peters said. Looking through the window at nothing in particular he murmured, 'The organisers have authorised me to negotiate up to a certain figure, but we'll keep that little piece of information to ourselves for the moment.'

The telephone rang and they all took their places.

'Mr Magnum, I presume,' Pete said, suddenly self-conscious at sounding like Mr Stanley greeting Doctor Livingstone.

'It's just MAGNUM,' the disembodied voice said impatiently. 'Shut up and listen. These are our terms. If you agree to them, we'll hand back the World Cup and return the dog in one piece. I don't think I need to go into the detail of what will happen if you don't.'

'What do you want?' Pete asked nervously.

'Half a million, in cash. Pack it in two bags, and leave it in the smallest police station in London at midnight tomorrow.'

'Wait, wait, slow down. Midnight tomorrow doesn't give us much time,' Pete complained.

'We'll be watching. No coppers, no surveillance.'

'What if we say no?'

'You have one chance. What's it going to be?'

'Okay, then, no.'

DC Palmer put his hand on the conference telephone speaker to mute it.

'What are you doing?'

'Calling his bluff,' Pete said loftily.

'You can call his bluff with someone else's dog,' Anwar said angrily.

'Tell him the trophy is a fake. Only used for display. That it's worthless and he's lost some of his bargaining power.'

Pete considered this for a moment and then did as he had been advised.

'Fake or not – and I think probably not and you're just desperate – we'll take that risk,' Jago said knowingly. 'If you don't meet the terms, the pooch gets it.'

'Don't you threaten me!' Pete Peters, who was used to getting his own way, lost his cool.

'DC Palmer here, Magnum,' Palmer cut in. 'How far do you boys think you're going to get?'

'Let us worry about that.'

'We have you bang to rights for the Northcote Road robbery, Jago. Is Finn there with you too, I wonder? You're both looking at a five-year stretch in prison.'

'It's all very well telling them they're guilty.' Sheena cut in having silenced the telephone. 'They know that already. We need to flush them out.'

'Say yes to their demands,' Anwar pleaded, searching the faces around him.

Sheena nudged Pete's knee under the table with hers.

'Just one moment, Magnum.' DC Palmer clicked the line off.

Sheena now raised her eyebrows at Pete and cocked her head to one side. She might have just as well shouted 'Oh, come on!' across the table. Pete stroked his chin in deliberation, as if looking for a misplaced beard.

'Give him something. I have an idea,' said Anwar.

Pete Peters' hand hovered over the telephone.

'All right, Magnum, we'll meet your terms,' he conceded. 'Where exactly is this small police station?'

'It is a small box on the southeast corner of Trafalgar Square. Midnight, tomorrow. We'll leave the dog and the trophy if the cash is there.' With that, the line went dead.
In the playground, Jago slid the back off his telephone and pulled out the SIM card.

'Job done, brother of mine,'

'We're in the money,' Finn sang tunelessly.

'You're right there. What's more, we'll be able to leave that madhouse.'

'Aw, it hasn't been that bad,' said Finn, and called Bonzo to him. 'I'll miss this little fella, too. He has such a lovely nature.' He scooped the little dog off the ground and gave him a hug.

'You've totally lost it, you know, you big softy.'

'You're fond of him as well, admit it.'

'He's pretty smart and a nice-enough-looking dog, I'll grant you that.'

'Nice-enough-looking? You hear what he's saying about you?' Finn held Bonzo's snout and talked to him the way people talk to babies 'You could be a film star, couldn't you, Bonzo? Couldn't you! Yes, you could!'

Jago shook his head in disbelief.

'Wonder dog or not, he's certainly got you under his spell. Come on, let's get him back to the house before someone spots him.'

If the brothers were feeling the strain of their situation, they weren't showing it. Meanwhile the mood in the World Cup office was not quite as positive.

'What now, mastermind?' Pete Peters asked Anwar. It seemed a tiny bit aggressive given that they were all on the same side.

'Just you hold on a minute.' Mr Bradfield stood up and jabbed a finger in Pete's direction. 'I think you should hear what he has to say before you start pointing fingers.' That made Mr Bradfield look at his own finger, which he then realised he was pointing. Sheepishly he withdrew it, as if holstering a gun.

Mr Bradfield's outburst took everyone by surprise, and a momentary silence descended on the small party.

'Actually, it was something Sheena said about flushing them out,' said Anwar. 'My wife and I were watching an old movie the other night, called *The Sting*. It occurred to me that we set up our own sting. You know, a trap for the crooks, so we can catch them in the act.'

'Hmm, I see your thinking,' said DC Palmer. 'We have to make sure we don't entice them to commit another crime. We're not allowed to that.'

'What we need to do is to get them to come to a place that we've chosen when they're off their guard.' Sheena was now warming to the plan.

'You mean give them tickets to a cinema or something and then pick them up when they use them.' Pete, having taken his telling-off, was back on side.

'That doesn't work because we don't know where they are to give them tickets.' Sheena seemed to have a better grip on how things would have to play out.

'We know their general location,' DC Palmer reminded them.

'What about advertising a dog show?' Mr Bradfield suggested.

'How many mutts will turn up to a dog show?' Pete Peters dismissed the idea.

'The cinema is an idea, though.' Sheena held up a finger as if to conduct incoming brainwaves. 'As Anwar said, we need to flush them out.'

'What, with a film?' Pete said dumbly.

'No, not with a film. *In* a film.' Sheena grinned. 'We advertise in the area for a dog to star in a short film. An advert, perhaps.'

'I get it. The star of the show will just happen to need all the qualities that match our Bonzo.'

'Precisely, Anwar. If we pitch it just right with the offer of a generous fee, then, if we're very lucky, we stand a chance,' Sheena concluded.

'It sounds like a plan. What do you think, DC Palmer?' Pete asked.

'I think it's a good idea. I can call in some favours and find us a location in Windsor.'

'Excellent. I'll deal with the local radio and TV,' volunteered Sheena.
'There's one small problem. We need to work fast. It needs to be done this afternoon. Something like this needs some creative input. A poster, flyers... How are we going to get that sorted?'

The others had to admit that this was an issue.

'I'm an illustrator,' said Anwar. 'I'll do it.' So everyone got to work.

Bernard Bradfield excused himself and made his way back to his office in the library. As he passed the East Gate entrance, he encountered a young man wandering uncertainly around. He was distinctive-looking, with an extraordinary pile of blond curls.

'May I help you?' Mr Bradfield asked.

'I'm looking for the Events Office. I was with a group but I just nipped into the loo and now I'm lost,' Muppet replied.

'Perhaps they thought they'd *loos* you.' Mr Bradfield was rather pleased with his joke.

Muppet gave him a look that suggested he was being weird.

'Herrrhem.' Mr Bradfield cleared his throat. 'I'm actually going that way myself. I'll show you.'

As they walked Mr Bradfield got over his awkwardness and made small talk.

'You're applying for a job, are you?'

'Just a temporary one to keep me out of trouble before I go back to college.'

'Ahh, you've been taking a break, have you?'

'You could say that,' Muppet said with an uneasy smile.

Bonzo the Wonder Dog and the Cricket World Cup

Before long they reached Mr Bradfield's destination.

'This is me,' he said, stopping at a pair of double doors. 'You just need to turn left after the arch and keep going straight.'

'I will, thank you,' Muppet replied.

The rest of the Toolbox Gang were doing nothing of the kind, and were still very much in business. But for how long would depend on how the plan was progressing.

Anwar had made a great job of the flyer. Across the top were the words APPLICANTS WANTED, and beneath them, URGENT CASTING CALL. Below that the page was divided into two areas. On the right a drawing of a dog bearing a passing resemblance to Bonzo being walked on a lead. On the left, Anwar had listed the details of the event.

Who? Compact, obedient, black-and-white dog
What? Casting of a would-be doggy TV star
Where? The Scout Hut, Willow Drive, Windsor
When? Friday 14th September 12-2pm
Why? Well-paid advertising campaign

Refreshments provided

'That's perfect,' Sheena said, leaning on the desk and scanning Anwar's handiwork. 'We'll email it through to Berkshire TV, the local news station. They've agreed to do a feature on it in the local bulletin after the six o'clock news today.'

'Is that it?' Pete complained. 'I've had to get special permission for all this expense, you know.'

'Several community radio stations are going to do a piece on it as well, and the police have agreed to distribute the flyers. In the time we have available, I think you'll be surprised at the reach we have.'

'What about social media?' Anwar asked.

'That may gather a momentum of its own. It's hard to predict.' As if to underline her point, Sheena's mobile phone buzzed on the desk. She held up a hand as if to quieten the others and took the call.

It was Kitty Karpati, a casting director. Sheena had reached out to her asking whether she would conduct the auditions. It was vital that the whole process appear as convincing as possible.

'Don't worry, hun, with my crew and their equipment we'll put on an Oscar-winning performance.'
'Great, that's brilliant. Thanks a million, Kitty, I owe you one,' Sheena concluded.

Later that afternoon the whole operation went live. From the small office, an entire network of volunteers was mobilised. The flyers were sent to a local print shop. The reporters of the print and screen media wrote their articles. Even Mr Hodges, who looked after the Scout Hut, gave it a jolly good sweep out. The casting crew assembled their kit and loaded it into their van ready for the next morning.

In the Royal Borough of Windsor, a similar vehicle had pulled up at the Mildwaters' B&B. The reversing beepers announced its arrival outside the building.

'Just sign here, madam,' the delivery driver said.

'Oh, right. I'll need my glasses.'

The delivery driver looked up to the heavens. He was on drop number sixty-four of a scheduled ninety-eight. Any unnecessary delay had a massive knock-on effect.

'Go on, I'll take that.' Finn, just back from the dog walk and pulling a fast one on the World Cup organisers, took the man's parcel. He signed an electronic pad with a squiggle and the delivery driver happily sped off.
'Where would you like this?' he said to Mrs Mildwater as she shuffled back.

'Has he gone? I was going to make him a cup of tea.'

'I think he was in a bit of a hurry, to be honest.'

'Thank you, dear. If you would bring it into the kitchen. It's a new television set. It seems our one was broken.'

'Of course, let me set it up for you.'

Finn felt a pang of guilt that the old people had broken into their pension to replace their perfectly good television. Although he did have to admit that he'd never seen a TV quite like their old one. Pebble-dashed with all sorts of kitchen substances, as if it was a stunt telly. Built to withstand everything the Mildwaters could throw at it.

Now, however, they had a pristine new set. Completely unboxed and assembled.

'I'll just tune it in for you and you'll be good to go.' Finn smiled at the old lady, who was clearly thrilled with her new purchase.

'That would be lovely, I have no idea about all that sort of thing and as for Cecil...' She tutted theatrically.

Finn worked the remote and put the television onto an 'autotune' setting. The set automatically scanned the airwaves. One after another the channels appeared as a static blur before blinking into a clear picture. Eventually, the programme had run its course.

'What would you like me to leave it on?' Finn asked.

'BBC One, please, dear. It's the news now. It'll only be that bloomin' Brexit, but the local news is on after and I always like to see that.'

'Shall I make you a nice cup of tea? After all, you look after my brother and me so nicely, it's the least I can do. Now, you sit down and put your feet up.'
Finn made the tea and together they watched the TV from the kitchen table.

'Now the news from where you are...' the newscaster announced.

'Tonight, on BBC Berkshire, why the cost of your commute is set to rise. A story of a local cat that has gone vegan. Also, are you wearing the wrong colour socks to work? A new in-depth study helps you to put your best foot forward. Then finally, a chance to hit the big time, if you've got the right looks of course – oh, and you're a dog. Then a look at what the weather has in store for us with Jasper Peacock. But first Lettuce the cat...'

'How ridiculous,' Mrs Mildwater grumbled at the television.

'The dog story sounds interesting,' Finn reasoned.

'Doggies!' Mrs Mildwater called.

There was a thundering of paws and a buffeting of the kitchen door. Mrs Mildwater opened it and two black Labradors burst in, followed at a more sedate pace by a third older dog with a grey muzzle.

'Ferris, Sloane, Cameron... SIT!' she commanded. Two of the dogs sat, followed by the third a beat later. The old lady rummaged in a jar behind the sink and tossed a dog treat to each of them in turn. They snapped up the treats and stayed rooted to the spot.

'That is impressive,' said Finn.

'They love a good dog story,' Mrs Mildwater explained.

'Now to a story with a difference,' the local news continued. 'Casting for a commercial is taking place in Windsor tomorrow. The director is looking for dogs to audition for a part in an upcoming advertising campaign that is to appear on television and other media outlets. Now, before the entire dog-owning population descends on the venue, do you fit the bill? The guidelines for the suitable applicant are quite specific. Candidates should be obedient black-and-white crossbreeds, no bigger than a medium-sized dog. So I'm afraid all you Great Dane and St Bernard owners need not apply. Potential applicants should attend the Scout Hut in Willow Drive between twelve and two tomorrow afternoon. What's the weather going to be like for the wannabe TV stars, Jasper?'

'Your Bernie should have a go,' Mrs Mildwater announced, in an unusual moment of clarity.

'I'm not sure Jago would like that, he's a very private person.'

'Nonsense, Bernie's just what they're looking for. You should give him a bath. Spruce him up for it.'

'I'll see what Jago says, but I wouldn't count on it.'

Later, up in their room, Jago's reaction was predictable.

'You've got to be joking?'

'You were just saying that he could be in the films.'

'That was before there was a chance he could be in a film!'

'He's a shoo-in for the job. Just think, we can make that extra bit of cash. Pay for that new telly them downstairs had to buy, for a start.'

'Listen to me.' Jago walked over to Finn and took him by the ears. 'You should have your head examined to think of such a daft thing.'

It seemed an over-reaction, and Finn was a bit ticked off.

'I'm going to take his nibs out for his pit-stop. Give you a break from my stupid ideas. Come on, Bonzo.'

The little dog was delighted to get another run-around. It had been a dry, bright day but as dusk fell, clouds spilled into the sky. The first fallen leaves of autumn blew about on a gust of wind. The same wind caught a paper that was stuck under the windscreen wiper of a car. Now free, the paper swirled about, landing at Finn's feet.

It was as if Anwar's flyer had been delivered to its intended recipient. Finn picked it up and scanned it.

What harm could it do? He thought.

Chapter 13 – Lights, Camera, Action!

Being in a police car was an odd sensation. Anwar wasn't sure if he was completely comfortable with it. Zak would have loved it, he knew that. It was better, though, that the children were left at school until this business was settled. If things went as planned then hopefully they would all be reunited at home that evening.

The clouds from the night before had delivered some light rain. It had spread from middle England and drifted south, arriving as a miserable drizzle. It was the sort of weather that kept voters away from elections.

The preparation of the Scout Hut had continued unabated throughout the morning. Eventually, the temporary studio was ready to receive its first hopeful candidates. Complete with a white background, umbrella lighting and camera crew, it looked completely authentic.

A small cast of players was assembled. None of them were playing themselves. Anwar, Sheena and DC Palmer were the representatives of Castigate Films. Each of them had been supplied with name badges showing suitably trendy job titles. Anwar, Artistic Ninja; Sheena, Brand Warrior; and Dave, Chief Amazement Officer. Pixie, Sheena's assistant, was posted on the main doors to meet and greet. Two police officers, in plain clothes and wearing radio earpieces, were positioned outside the front door. Finally, Mr Hodges was stationed at the side door. With their roles all sorted out, the 'crew' took their places and awaited the result of their brief shout-out to the canine world.

For the brothers, it was a potentially life-changing day. If all went well, they'd have enough money for a fresh start. If not, then the future looked less bright. A continued existence on the run or a 'Go Directly to Jail' card. No passing 'Go', no collecting half-a-million pounds.

Their plan wasn't the most complex ever devised. It relied on trust, timing and an element of good fortune. The same could be said of both sides of the equation. The World Cup organisers would have their fair share of misgivings and would also be jittery.

'I'm not keen on using the old banger for this evening,' Jago confessed.

'It's a bit late now.'

'What about the boy, the driver? The puppet?'

'Muppet,' Finn corrected him. 'I think you've well and truly scared him off.'

'We only need to get there, I guess. We lie low overnight and get some new wheels tomorrow.'

There was a creak on the landing floorboards outside their door. Mr Mildwater was pottering around. There was a lot of tutting and eventually he made his way downstairs.

'Have you seen my favourite cardigan, dearest?' he asked his wife when he met her in the kitchen.

'I put that smelly old thing in the garage, I'm afraid.'

As this was a regular occurrence he thanked her and made his way outside. Like the rest of the house, the garage had seen better days. The old wooden double doors stuck and he had to lift one of them on its hinge to get it open. He grunted with the effort and pushed it to one side. He was surprised to find the old Morris Minor in the garage. He'd sold his own car some months previously because of his age, and had got used to the empty space.

'What a lovely old thing,' he said, admiring the little car. 'I remember when Marigold and I had one just like this.' He put his hand on the bonnet and leaned on it, then looked at the number plate and murmured, 'SPD 111.' Suddenly invigorated, he pushed open the other garage door. The car was now entirely recognisable.

'Well, I never!' he said out loud, clasping his hands in front of him. 'I don't believe it!' he cried. There, in his garage, was the car that he and Marigold had owned when they first got married.

He edged round to the side and tried the driver's door. It opened, and he eased himself into the driver's seat. As he wrapped his fingers around the steering wheel, the years fell away. He ran his hand over the passenger seat. The aged leather had a smell that transported him back to another time. He pulled the glove-box door open, and there were the keys. He weighed them in his hand. Just starting her up wouldn't hurt, surely. He selected the ignition key and turned the engine over. On the third attempt, the little car fired up.

'Did you hear that?' Finn asked Jago.

'Hear what?'

'That sounded like the car.'

'Of course it was a car, we're right on a road.'

Finn looked out of the window and scanned both up and down the road.

Inside the garage, Mr Mildwater revved the engine gently. He felt rejuvenated by it, and he put the car in gear, lowered the handbrake and edged out of the garage. Finn was just about to turn away when he saw the nose of the old green car.

'It's our car. The old codger's only gone and taken it out of the garage.'

'What, Mr Mildwater? I wouldn't have thought he had it in him.'

'Well, he has, and he's in it! Quick!'

But Mr Mildwater wasn't just taking the car out of the garage. Now that he had the bit between his teeth there was no stopping him.

Inside the house, the two brothers scrabbled clumsily for the door of the bedroom.
'Don't leave the dog, we can't lose both our bargaining tools,' Jago barked.

Time spent resting had given Jago's foot a chance to improve a bit. Despite his boot, he was able to move more freely. Mr Mildwater was making slow and shaky progress down the road.

The brothers gave chase. He wasn't going to break any land-speed records but, annoyingly, he was going just too fast for them to catch up with him.

****

At the Scout Hut, a surprisingly long queue had formed down Willow Drive. Windsor was apparently full of aspiring doggy stars.

A makeshift curtain had been hung in front of the entrance. Pixie stuck her head through it, looking anxious.

'There are quite a lot of them out here, and they're starting to get restless.'

'Do the guys on the door have their photos of the suspects?' Sheena checked with DC Palmer.

'Of course. And of Bonzo,' he added.

'In that case, let's have our first "auditionee",' Sheena replied, making airborne inverted commas. 'Places, everyone.'

Anwar took his place behind the camera. He was wearing a baseball cap and dark glasses, partly to complete the look, and partly to disguise him. DC Palmer installed himself behind a small desk and adopted an expression that suggested he was hard to impress. Mr Hodges braced himself at the side door to eject the rejected applicants.

Pixie consulted her clipboard. 'This is err... Satan,' she said, sounding slightly anxious.

A muscular, shorthaired black-and-white mutt dragged its owner forcibly through the curtain.

'Where would you like us?' Satan's nervy-looking owner asked.

'On the little table in front of the backdrop, if you would?' Sheena replied in a no-nonsense tone. There followed a bit of energetic wrestling, which Satan won. It resulted in nobody sitting on the table and a cry of 'NEXT!' from DC Palmer. Mr Hodges saw them off the premises with the minimum amount of fuss and no bloodshed. As the door closed on Satan, the curtain at the front of the building billowed and parted again.

'Mrrrowww.' The next applicant introduced herself.

'Is that a cat?'

'Yes, but a very big one.'

'NEXT!'

An enormous 'BOWGH, WAWGH!' accompanied a compact Jack Russell called Brutus. He was obedient and sat nicely to have his photo taken.

'Have you given the young lady your details?' Anwar asked, looking up from behind the camera. The owner nodded.

'Thank you, we'll be in touch.'

This pleasant, easy-going interaction made Mr Hodges' job that much easier, though he was still worried Satan would be back, after his dismissal had required a degree of strong-arming.

A black-and-white Schnauzer called Pongo had a similar reaction to him. After starting out totally placid, he began snarling and baring his teeth when confronted with the hapless doorman.

Throughout the audition, the procession continued. The *tik*, *tik*, *tik* of claws on the Scout Hut floor. The accompanying 'Yap!' 'Yelp!' 'Ruff!' and the cry of 'NEXT!'

Too black, too white, too big, too small. Too badly behaved. Too 'meh'. So many hopefuls. The 'Waaf, waff' of a puppy and the 'Wuff, wuff' of a more senior auditionee.

Pixie looked through the curtains again. There was a different, but still worried, look on her face as she asked.

'Do we have a poop bag?'

The auditionees were friendly, happy to have their stab at getting into the limelight. The dogs were generally an easy-going lot too, and the *fwip, fwip* of wagging tails added to the background noise. Some had to be coaxed into it; Prince the poodle for one was definitely not keen. Meanwhile, Dorrit, a young lurcher, enjoyed the warmth of the lights so much that she had to be lifted off the table. But there was still no sign of the real star of the show.

DC Palmer stretched his legs and walked down the remainder of the queue outside. He nodded his greetings to the prospective hopefuls and scanned them for the brothers and Bonzo.

'No sign of them,' he said to Sheena back in the hut. Perhaps it was just too much of a long shot.'

'It was a good turn-out and worth a go. Are there many left?

'Just a few more.'

****

Mr Mildwater had made slow progress around the town. The Morris Minor was still going and more importantly was still intact. The brothers had been able to keep up by cutting corners wherever they could. As a result, they had managed to keep him in their sights. Now a hill threatened to slow him down sufficiently for them to overtake.

Oblivious to his pursuers, Mr Mildwater was just delighting in being reunited with his old car. He was also unaware that as it climbed the hill the car was slowing down to a halt.

'There,' Jago gasped. 'The old devil is slowing down to a standstill. We'll nab him before he gets to the end of this street.'

Eventually, the car stalled completely. Jago, Finn and Bonzo arrived just as it did.

'Gotcha!' Jago cried in triumph.

'Eh, what?' Cecil Mildwater replied vaguely.

'You took our car,' Jago boomed at the old man.

'My apologies. You see...' The old man went into a long-winded explanation.

Finn let his thoughts drift as the old boy told the story of the car. The sign taped to the building next to him brought him back down to earth.

'DOG AUDITION TODAY'

'Hey, Jago, would you look at that? The dog audition, it's right here. I'll just ask those two fellas.'

'NO,' Jago said, registering the sign. 'Definitely not.'

'Aw, go on.'

'I'm warning you...'

With that, Finn swept up Bonzo and nipped between the two men standing sentry at the door. They exchanged a knowing glance as he and Bonzo passed between them.

Finn was immediately plunged into darkness.

'Helloo?' he called out.

'We're in here,' Pixie replied. 'We thought we'd finished for the day.'

'Are we too late?'

'Not at all. Come in.'

As Finn entered the room, Sheena did a neat pirouette, taking in Anwar and Dave Palmer with a triumphant smile.

'Welcome,' she purred. 'Who do we have here?'

'Bernie,' Finn replied. 'I heard your request on the local news. I have to say I think he's a dead cert for the role.'

'I have a feeling that he's just the little dog we are looking for...'

'Do I put him on here?' Finn gestured to the table against the white background.

'You do indeed.' DC Palmer got to his feet and edged round to block Finn's exit.

Finn placed Bonzo on the table. As soon as he did so, the little dog started barking.

'This is most unlike him, he doesn't usually...'

'Bow-wow, wow, wow, wow!' Bonzo let rip with an astonishing bout of sustained barking before launching himself off the table. With one bound he vaulted the camera and landed on Anwar's lap, knocking off his baseball cap and sunglasses. The little dog placed his paws on his owner's shoulders and gave him a thorough and prolonged licking.

On seeing Anwar, Finn executed the most stupendous double-take, and bolted. DC Palmer had already predicted this and blocked his way. Undaunted, Finn made a neat side-step and ran to the other end of the Scout Hut. Unfortunately, he had not counted on Mr Hodges and his trusty broom being in place. He was felled by it striking him just below the knee.

'Suspect down,' DC Palmer radioed through to his colleagues.

Now their suspicions were confirmed, the two policemen moved in on Jago.

'May we have a word with you, sir?'

'Get out of the car,' Jago ordered Mr Mildwater roughly.

'What?' the old man stuttered.

'Get out!' Jago grabbed him forcibly.

Mr Mildwater may have been old and a bit doddery, but he would not be treated in this way. 'Unhand me, young man!' he exclaimed indignantly. 'I am quite capable of exiting the vehicle.' With a supreme effort, he wrenched himself from the seat. Then with a flamboyant wave of his hand he invited Jago to take the wheel. Jago climbed in and made to start the car, but the old boy had been too quick for him and had taken the keys from the ignition. Jago banged the wheel with both hands in frustration.

'Keys?' he demanded of the old man, motioning with an open palm.
'These?' Mr Mildwater replied, casually tossing them into a nearby hedge.

'Why, you...!' Jago scrambled out of the car and grabbed the old man roughly. 'What did you do that for, you silly old fool?' Mr Mildwater wriggled in his grip.

The two policemen, uncertain of how things might develop, bounced on their toes like a pair of goalies. If Jago fled, they were prepared to set off after him in any direction.

Mr Mildwater, however, was proving quite a handful. As they continued to wrestle, the old man wriggled out of his tweed jacket, leaving Jago holding it by the empty arms. During the struggle, he'd pulled a cord from the pocket. Attached to it was his dog whistle, and as he spun away from his assailant, he blew it for all he was worth.

Inside the Scout Hut, Bonzo, who was still busy getting reacquainted with Anwar, pricked up an ear. The shrill whistle was just a tiny peep to the human ear, but to Bonzo, it was a full-blown foghorn. The little dog leaped from Anwar's lap and bolted out through the front door.

Out on the street, the policemen had decided on their course of action. They were executing a well-orchestrated pincer movement, edging around the car to cut Jago off. He, however, had other plans, and seeing that they had played their hand he nipped back into the car. Sliding across the driver's seat, negotiating the gear stick, and slipping into the passenger seat, he was in the process of making good his escape. He banged the passenger door closed behind him with a triumphant shout of 'AHA!' and prepared to sprint off.

At this moment Bonzo shot out of the building like a low-flying missile. He connected with the spot just behind Jago's knee. He went flying spectacularly, base over apex, before landing in a bewildered heap.

The policemen, who had reversed their pincer movement, arrived to fit the obligatory handcuffs.

'All right, it's a fair cop,' he muttered, surrendering to his fate. 'What you're looking for is in there. It's all yours, take it away, fill yer boots!'

He nodded towards the back of the little car as the policeman got him to his feet.

Bonzo, for his part, was scampering breathlessly up and down the pavement. He paused for a moment to be stroked by Mr Mildwater.

'You're a clever chap,' the old man said as he gave his woolly head a rub. That was nice enough, but clearly, to Bonzo's mind, the stupendous doggy-alert he'd responded to had been a false alarm. Satisfied that all was right with the world again, he trotted back inside the hut to find Anwar.

In the hut, Finn was sitting on a long bench against the back wall, looking shamefaced. The reunion between Bonzo and Anwar had been touching, and even the hardest heart couldn't help but be affected.

'I feel pretty awful when you see that,' Finn admitted to his brother, who had been sat next to him.

Anwar put Bonzo on the floor and attached his lead.

'There's nothing special about that mutt, you know. He's just somebody's pet, plain and simple. Remember, you can say something totally daft to a dog and he'll look at you as if you're the smartest guy in the world. This one is no different to any other. A bowl of nibbles and a walk around the block is all he aspires to in a day. And there we were thinking we'd get us some wonder dog.'

'Come on, you two,' DC Palmer said. 'You've got some explaining to do back at the station. Like how you thought you'd get away with this crackpot scheme, for starters.'

As the brothers were led past Anwar and Bonzo, they paused.

'Goodbye, little fella, we had some good times,' Finn said.

'Aw go'wan, will ya,' Jago scolded his brother. Bonzo looked back at the men. In particular, he held Jago's eye. Jago stared back and for a moment thought the dog had winked at him. *No, surely not.* He shook his head to banish the thought. But the dog had *definitely* winked...

With that, the brothers were led away to a waiting police car.

After relieving the police of the trophy, Mr Hodges set it down on the dog's casting table. Now framed in the camera's viewfinder, its image flashed up captured on the camera's screen. Sheena, who was feeling pretty pumped, stood behind the camera.

'That looks pretty good to me. Well done, you,' she congratulated Anwar. 'A brilliant idea skilfully carried out.'

'I'm just glad it's all over. I'm looking forward to getting the family together and putting this all behind us.'

'Surely not. This is just the beginning,' Sheena enthused.

'This is the end of the beginning, full stop.'

'Do you think we could at least get a picture of Bonzo with the cup?'

'I think we could just about manage that,' Anwar replied with a grin, his reluctance melting away.

Chapter 14 – The World Cup Goes Off with a Bang

The photo taken that afternoon was one that the British public came to associate with their new national hero. 'Bonzo saves the Cricket World Cup', read the headlines.

Summer was over, we'd failed to win the Football World Cup and the news was either Trumped up or Brexity. Bonzo's image appeared across the media. Shared, Tweeted, Whatsapped, Snapchatted, Instagrammed. It captured something, a feel-good moment. The spirit of the good old plucky Brit. 'Are we downhearted? Not when we have dogs like Bonzo around.'

Where *was* their hero, though? After their previous experience, the Khans had firmly turned down all offers to appear in the media.

Bonzo's return to the family home had been a momentous event. His disappearance had been overwhelming in many ways. One day, out of the blue, he had been taken from them. The pain of knowing that he was somewhere else going about his usual everyday stuff had been difficult for any of them to bear. Then suddenly he was home, in his bed, pulling bits off his toys, pointing out mealtimes, waiting expectantly by the door. They would never take him for granted again.

At Lord's Cricket Ground, Mr Saad had appeared with indecent haste to collect the World Cup. It suggested that his confidence in letting anyone else take care of the trophy had been damaged. Much like the trophy itself, he might have pointed out.

'Clearly, I'll be back in the new year as the big day of the opening ceremony gets nearer. In the meantime, I think we'll be sending over the replica for your promotional events.'

Sheena and Pete Peters had been the winners in the whole affair. The profile of the upcoming competition had been given a tremendous boost by the media coverage. It was comparable to the run-up to the London Olympics. Once the public interest had been sparked, it had built, and the pair were keen to make the most of this trend.

'Are you sure we can't get the little dog involved?' Pete pleaded.

'The owners are absolutely adamant.'

'They can't say no to the opening ceremony, surely?'

Sheena weighed the idea in her mind, and agreed. 'Probably not.'

A couple of days later an envelope printed with the logo of the World Cup plopped through the letterbox of the Khan home.

'Hey, Dad, what do you think this is?' Zak asked.

'Who's it addressed to?'

'Everyone. Even Bonzo.'

'But Bonzo can't read,' Lita observed. She was going through a stage of taking things just a bit too literally.

'Lighten up, Lita,' Zak scolded her. It was he who was suffering most from the current fad.

'I think whoever it's from is just being polite,' said Anwar, taking the envelope. He'd already guessed its contents. 'Hey, we've been invited to attend the opening ceremony and the first game of the World Cup.'

The two children pressed him to show them the tickets. 'How cool. And it's just down the road from us at the Oval.'

Inside, there was also a letter addressed to Jen and Anwar.

'Dear Mr and Mrs Khan,

We totally respect your decision to distance yourself from the events relating to the theft of the World Cup. However, it is impossible to ignore your role in securing its return. As such we wonder whether we might involve you in some small way in the opening ceremony on 30 May 2019...'

There was more detail regarding the need to attend some rehearsals if they agreed to take part.

'What do you think?' Anwar asked Jen later.

'We've been saying no to everything,' Jen pointed out. 'But it would be kind of special to get involved in a big global event like this.'

Therefore it was decided that when the time came, they would, within reason, take part in whatever it was the organisers had cooked up for them.

****

The call came at the end of March. Anwar had to attend the Oval Cricket Ground with Bonzo a couple of times.

'What does he have to do, Dad?' asked Lita.

'He just has to sit there and look beautiful, sweetie.'

'He has to practice that?'

'It's a secret. You'll see.'

Of course, saying that something was a secret didn't put an end to the questions. In fact, it only led to broader speculation about what it was that Bonzo was going to be doing.

However, the time passed as the kids counted down the calendar. The excitement of more school holidays distracted them and then came the start of a new term. April brought some much-needed sunshine back into everyone's lives and in due course the morning of May the thirtieth arrived.

It would be a day of memorable events for the children, starting with a prized day off school. Clearly, being a part of a global event taking place practically on their own doorstep ran that a close second. The Oval Cricket Ground has a Tube station nearby and the Khan family only had to travel four stops to get there. Bonzo, as ever, took such things in his stride. He liked the attention that people paid him. He also got a good ride in Anwar's arms on the escalator.

When they resurfaced on Harleyford Road, they found the area buzzing with people looking to meet friends, buy picnic food or pick up their team's colours from the many traders who had temporarily set up shop on the pavements.

Jen consulted the instruction sheet that had accompanied their tickets.

'It says that we should enter through the Jack Hobbs Gates.' These were the main gates in front of the old red brick pavilion, named after a famous England cricketer. The children knew who he was because he'd once lived in the next road along from theirs. There was a commemorative blue plaque fixed to his house, and Anwar had looked him up on Wikipedia.

There was a steward checking people's tickets at the gate. He was taking his job very seriously.

'You should take the children through the turnstiles, madam,' he instructed tersely.

'Actually, we have these special identity passes,' Jen explained politely but firmly.

The steward inspected their passes and immediately changed his tune.

'Absolutely, madam, go straight ahead.'

The family group made their way through the gate.

'Hang on, you can't bring that dog in here.' The steward started up again.

'He has his own special pass too,' Anwar explained. He picked up Bonzo and showed the steward the tag attached to his collar. 'VIP' was printed in large black letters with a note underneath it: 'Access all areas including pitch.'

'I've not seen one of those before. Would you hang on a moment?' The steward checked with his supervisor on his walkie-talkie. Then his tone shifted up another gear, from consenting to positively reverential.

'Please go straight ahead, and please accept my sincere apologies for the delay. Go straight ahead and up the stairs. There'll be some there to take care of you.'

'That's more like it, he's a Very Important Pooch,' said Anwar to Jen as they walked away before bursting out laughing. It was the first time any of them had been treated in such a swanky way. The five-star treatment was something the Khans felt they could get used to, particularly as more spectators arrived. The forecourt in front of the building was teeming with people going this way and that. The family threaded their way through the crowd but were stopped by someone calling out to them. Or, more precisely, to their dog.

'Oi, Bonzo!'

The whole family looked around to where the shout had come from. All they could see was an ice-cream kiosk.

'Yes, over here!'

'Sorry, do we know you?' Anwar asked the ice-cream salesman.

Bonzo was going through all the motions that suggested that he knew and liked this person.

'Hello, Bonzo. Have you been a good boy?' he asked.

The family still looked utterly puzzled.

'Sorry. I'm Finn, one –' he leaned as close to them as possible and whispered – 'one of the kidnappers.'

'The what?!' exclaimed Jen.

'I'm out of jail on a special tag,' he explained. 'The judge felt I'd been led astray by my domineering brother and I have to prove I've turned over a new leaf.'

'That's good to hear,' Anwar admitted. 'I have to say, Bonzo had been well cared for, so you can't be all bad.'

'He's a lovely little chap. You're fortunate to have him.'

It was the sort of conversation that could have gone on for some time without actually going anywhere.

'We must get on. We wish you luck, Mr, err...Finn,' Jen let the words drift away and led the children briskly towards the stairs. Here they were shown to a lift that in turn took them up to the organisers' corporate box.

In the Richie Benaud Box, the family were treated like long-lost friends. All their past contacts were there: Pete, Sheena and Mr Bradfield. Even DC Palmer had the day off to join in the celebration and to see the tournament get underway.

In a country with unpredictable weather, today's was unpredictably good. Better than the organisers, in their wildest dreams, could have imagined. The Oval Cricket Ground was manicured to perfection. The spectators, who might lift the event to another level, filed into their seats, buzzing with expectation. The view was magnificent, with the vast sweep of the stand in front of them. The playing surface was decked out for the opening ceremony, with the backdrop of the London skyline beyond. There's nothing quite like actually being at a great sporting event.

'Have you ever been here before?' Sheena asked Zak.

'We've all been to a T20. It wasn't nearly as cool as this, we weren't high up so you couldn't see everything.' He gestured at the view.

'I liked the mascot best,' Lita added.

'In that case, you'll probably enjoy the opening ceremony.'

'We've seen the Olympic Opening Ceremony online. Do you think the Queen will arrive by parachute?'

'That was a few years ago. I think her parachuting days are behind her. But there's bound to be the odd surprise.'

Sheena drifted away, allowing the children to investigate the goody bags they'd received. She joined Pete Peters, who was making small talk with Jen and Anwar. He was in his natural habitat, at his smarmy best. Bonzo's lead dangled from Anwar's right hand. The dog had splayed himself on the ground and adopted a bored expression.

'May I just borrow Anwar for a moment?' Sheena asked the group.

The two of them broke away and Sheena spoke to him quietly.

'We'll be calling you in half an hour or so, if that's all right with you.'

'Sure, that's great.' He nodded and re-joined his wife.

'What was that about?' Jen asked as he edged in next to her.

'You'll see,' he smiled.

Beneath them in the bowels of the building, Billy Murphy – Muppet to his shady acquaintances – was late for work.

'Where have you been?' the Artistic Director demanded, tapping his watch. 'Everyone else is changed and ready to go.'

'Sorry,' Muppet pleaded. 'I had no idea it would be so busy. It's taken me ages to get out of the Tube station.'

'The clue is in the title: World Cup. One or two people were going to show,' the director batted back sarcastically. 'I knew it was a mistake giving him the role,' he said to his assistant Milly, who was hovering by his side.

'To be fair, he was the only volunteer for the position, if you'll remember,' Milly pointed out.

He swatted her away. In his mind, the boy's inclusion had been a disaster waiting to happen.

For his part, now that he was there, Muppet was determined to make up for the past. He emerged from the changing room after putting on his costume in double quick time. The makeover was extraordinary. Muppet's slight frame had been turned into something much fuller – almost fat, one might say. A fat-suit, a wig, a cap and a big beard completed the transformation.

He took his place at the back of a line of ten motorised red circular floats, each of them topped with a scene depicting a famous cricketing event. The players of the ten teams now took their place, lining up in the tunnel beneath the stadium's seating. They were resplendent in their team caps and blazers, each one led by a flag-bearing mascot.

Inside the stadium, the spectators were prepared for the start of the ceremony. The public address system boomed out the announcer's introduction.

'Welcome to the Oval and the London opening ceremony of the Cricket World Cup!'

The crowd gave a spontaneous cheer.

'Here we go,' Sheena said, rubbing her hands. This was the culmination of a lot of hard work and planning for everyone involved.

A series of flares went off in sequence around the stadium, and the first of the motorised floats emerged from beneath the stands. The large red disc viewed from the stands looked like a giant cricket ball rolling slowly around the outfield. It was topped with a depiction of Hambledon Cricket Club, which was popularly known as 'the cradle of cricket'.

Behind it the England cricketers, the hosting team, marched out behind the cross of St George. Next, the first Test Match between England and Australia, followed by the Australian team.

In the box, Anwar gave Sheena a nudge.

'I think Bonzo and I should get going.'

'Absolutely. I'll get someone to take you down.'

Jen and the kids had moved to the seats outside the box. Here they could make the most of their spectacular vantage point. They assumed Anwar was just being slow and didn't notice him slip away with Bonzo.
Milly was waiting for them in the corridor.

'It's Mr Khan and Bonzo, isn't it?' She bent down and gave the dog a stroke. 'We're ready for you downstairs if you'd like to follow me.'

They walked with her along the corridor to the lifts. A security guard had called one and was holding the door open for them. From there they were whisked down several levels to a control room in the bowels of the stadium. From here the whole staging of the event was being masterminded.

Out on the pitch, the floats continued with the theme of the women's game. Various well-known female players waved to the crowds. They were wearing clothing that showed the development in the game's dress. These ranged from flouncy white dresses of the Victorian age through to the coloured branded uniforms of today. The New Zealand team marched behind the float in neat formation. They passed a stand where members of the so-called Beige Brigade, the New Zealand supporters group, were situated. One member was particularly vocal in his support.

'GO ON, YOU BLACK CAPS!' he shouted. It was Loud Dunc, putting his considerable expertise in being LOUD to good use.

Next, the Indian sub-continental teams of Pakistan, Sri Lanka and India had floats that led out their teams. Each nation had previously won the competition and the date of their tournament win made up the central theme of their displays. The fast bowlers and dominance of Brian Lara's and Viv Richards bat were highlighted for the West Indies. Then there was the celebration of the 1992 reintroduction of South Africa to international competition.

The growth of the international game was represented with floats for Afghanistan and Bangladesh both relative new-comers to the international stage. The whole spectacle focused on the development of the game and its diversity. A message that people aren't all the same, but they can come together through cricket. There were positive messages everywhere.

By now all the teams and all the floats were out on the pitch. Slowly the teams broke away from the circle and lined up in front of the old Victorian Pavilion. In the middle of the ground, a podium had been rolled into place. On it the seventies pop band 10CC had come together to give a rousing rendition of their hit 'Dreadlock Holiday'. The words were flashed up on the big screens with a bouncy karaoke ball picking out the lyrics. This enabled the spectators to blast out the subtitled words: 'We don't like cricket, WE LOVE IT!'

The band was expertly spirited away by well-drilled volunteers and the announcer introduced the next item.

'In the history of the game, there can be few more recognisable characters than our next cricketer.'

Jaunty brass-band music played over the speaker system, and Muppet, standing backstage, was given a prod. He duly complied and marched from the darkness of the stands into the bright London sunshine. As he emerged, it was clear who he was playing. With his trademark beard, fat tummy and brightly coloured cap there was no mistaking W.G. Grace. Muppet strode about in a pompous and theatrical way. No doubt the 'Old Man' of English cricket would not have been impressed. However, this depiction was meant in a light-hearted way and the crowd got behind him.

At one end of the ground, a set of huge three-metre-high stumps had been set up. They obscured Cecil Mildwater's view of the pitch but he didn't much care. He had taken refuge behind his newspaper, content to sit out whatever was going on until play began.

The W.G. Muppet strode over to the stumps and picked up a bat that had been leaning against them. While he made a great performance of swishing it about, the middle stump was slowly lowered to a forty-five-degree angle. A ladder was produced and propped up against it. It was clear that it was hollow, and W.G. Grace was going to climb into it.

As he made his way up the ladder, the brass-band music faded and a crescendo of drumroll replaced it. W.G. made it to the top of the ladder and gave the crowd a wave with his bat, then disappeared. The drumroll stopped and a hush descended over the grounds.

The public address system crackled into life.

'Ladies, gentleman and children, let's give W.G. Grace a big cheer for his biggest ever six!'

With that, the hollow stump belched a cough of smoke, and a resounding bang launched Muppet into the air. From the other side of the ground, a football-sized red cricket ball was simultaneously launched.

Having been fired from the cannon Muppet's trajectory took a pleasing arc. As he reached the top of it, he appeared to hang in the air momentarily. For an instant he contemplated the stadium, the ground and the thousands of faces turned skywards. Was that the London Eye he could see? However, he had a job to do, and he'd needed to have his wits about him. Ah, here it was, right on cue.

As the ball travelled towards him, he met it with a full swing of the bat. The contact was thin – in a game he'd have been caught by first slip – but the *BOOM* was resounding. Below him, the podium had been cranked up, and its top opened. As the bat connected with it, a great cloud of exploding ball-bits heralded the unveiling of the Cricket World Cup Trophy and its unlikely rescuer. There, elevated high above the stadium, was Bonzo the Wonder Dog (oh, and Anwar).

As Muppet sailed over the podium and landed in a safety net, Lita and Zak were delighted by the spectacle. Both of them jumped to their feet and cried 'It's Bonzo, it's our Bonzo!'

The opening had been a resounding success. Now complete, the playing surface was cleared for the game. The TV companies rolled out their equipment, their pitch-side helpers and commentators. The England and South African players returned to the wicket now ready to do battle, while the spectators settled down for the first game of the competition.
Bonzo and Anwar arrived back in the box, and everyone clapped them. Anwar's face bore the after-effects of the ball explosion and Bono had a pink tinge to his white fur.

'Hello, my superstar boys,' Jen enthused. 'How exciting was that?'

'Actually, it was a bit nerve-wracking. We seemed to be squashed in that podium for an age.'

'Come and sit down and watch the game.'

Anwar eased himself into the seat next to Jen, leaving Bonzo sitting on a step in the aisle. Several of the other guests in the box were keen to make a fuss of the little dog. Soon other members of the crowd started to notice that he was there. Their waving soon caught the attention of the TV director. The camera swung round to where they were sitting and soon the family was framed on the big screens suspended around the pitch.

'Hey, look,' Zak cried. 'It's us!'

The whole family waved together.

Back in his studio, the director barked the command, 'We need the dog! Zoom in the dog!'

The camera panned around the box before finally spotting Bonzo on the step. The cameraman zoomed in until the little dog was fully framed on every screen around the ground. A caption appeared at the bottom of the screen: 'Bonzo, finder of the Cricket World Cup'.

In that instant, for everyone in the ground to see, Bonzo winked.

The End

CPSIA information can be obtained
at www.ICGtesting.com
Printed in the USA
BVHW070920050619
550220BV00002B/212/P